A VALIANT KNOX NOVEL

Jess Anastasi

Entangled Publishing, LLC
2614 South Timberline Road
Suite 109
Fort Collins, CO 80525
Visit our website at www.entangledpublishing.com.

Select Otherworld is an imprint of Entangled Publishing, LLC.

Edited by Robin Haseltine
Cover design by Brittany Marczak
Photography by iStock

Manufactured in the United States of America

First Edition February 2015

Lisa
You introduced me to the romance genre, became my best friend, the older sister I never had, and someone to throw crazy ideas around with or talk books for hours. Without you, I definitely wouldn't be where I am today.

Chapter One

MAY, 2436
ILARI, BRANNON SYSTEM

The precise scratches on the wall across from him tapered off into a dim blur toward the far corner of the cell where the light didn't quite reach. There were far more marks than Kai wanted to count. Time had distorted into an immeasurable haze ever since the heavy, steel-reinforced door had clanged shut and locked behind him. Having a record of how long he'd been in here made his skin crawl, but damned Amos had carefully scored a new mark every time the sun came up and sent a teasing shaft of golden light through the paneless barred slit of a window.

Kai shivered under his ragged coat and breathed in the hint of fresh coldness over the revolting dank and rotting dungeon-esque smells. The brief slant of sunlight made an appearance and he lifted his head to look over at Amos, huddled on his side against the opposite wall. Any second now, his friend would sit up and drag himself over to add another score to the tally.

Muffled banging echoed from outside the cell. Slop time, right when the sun came up, just like every other goddamn morning he'd awakened here.

"Amos, get your lazy ass up. No sleeping in on my time, Sergeant."

The door to their cell made a series of clicking noises and then swung outward, but Amos didn't move.

Two black-robed figures appeared in the doorway. One stood back while the other walked in and dropped two bowls of gray swill in the middle of the rough concrete floor.

"Enjoy your breakfast, Commander." The one in the doorway sneered. "And don't forget to pray before you start. The Lord God is watching."

Kai clenched his jaw over the words "screw you and your psychotic religion" but that'd only get him another beat-down, just like it had the other twenty or so times he'd lost his temper and opened his mouth.

The two men left and slammed the door behind them. He let his head fall back against the cold cement wall and fortified his mental defenses to endure another meal of goo that tasted like manure. Eating the stuff had become a lottery for the damned. Some days it made them so sick they'd barely get it down before it came back up again. Sometimes the slop was drugged and it'd knock them out cold for a few hours. Mostly it just tasted bad and left him feeling queasy. But refusing to eat it was not an option, not if he wanted to survive.

With a determined exhale, he sat forward and braced for

the pain of moving his damaged leg. A couple of a-holes had broken it early on in his confinement, and without any type of medical attention, the bones hadn't healed right. He could still get around on it, but if any of the Christ's Sunday Soldier jerks wanted to torture him, all they needed to do was get him to walk laps of his cell. The ache would be all right for a while, but eventually he'd start sweating and getting light-headed from the pain. Of course, being half-starved and dehydrated didn't help any.

With a sideways dragging kind of movement, he shuffled over to the two bowls, which also put him in poking range of Amos. *Lazy sonuvabitch*. He'd missed the whole three minutes worth of sun they got to see every day.

"Come on, grub's up. It's a four-star serving of crud. With any luck it won't be poisoned today."

Amos still didn't respond and with a muttered curse at having to move farther, Kai lugged himself over to his sergeant and grabbed the man's shoulder.

"Wake up." He shook him, gentle at first, and then harder when the guy didn't rouse. A spike of gut-clenching apprehension took hold deep within him as he rolled Amos over.

The sergeant's lips were blue, his skin waxy and gray.

No.

He slapped a trembling hand to Amos's neck, searching for a pulse, for a sign of breathing, any little spark of hope. But he felt nothing except the rubbery post-rigor-mortis flesh of a dead man.

"No!" The hoarse yell ripped deep from within his chest as he pounded a fist down on the sergeant's shoulder. The impact jarred his hand as he struck bone. He focused on the pain, drawing in short ragged breaths as his lungs seized.

Since the religious zealots had grabbed him and Amos, each day had been a living hell. But the two of them had strengthened each other, had made a pact to survive and get home. Except Amos was dead, and inside, Kai could feel himself crumbling.

He sucked in another strangled breath and turned away from the body, only to come face to face with all those goddamn marks on the wall. Fury blazed, burning through him like a sun going supernova.

Reaching down, he found Amos's limp, cold hand. "I can't believe you up and goddamn died on me, Sergeant. Cutting out wasn't an option. I'm sure as hell not spending another night here, not alone. When those CSS dicks come back for the bowls, I'm taking them down and whatever happens after that…"

His mind went blank and he tightened his hold on the sergeant's icy hand. It didn't take a genius to work out what would happen if he went on the attack. Beneath his fingers, the bones of Amos's hand dug into his palm. No, not bone. Alloy. A few years back, his friend's hand and most of his arm up past the elbow had been crushed. Nearly all of the bones had been replaced with a lightweight alloy.

He glanced down at the hand and then over to the vacant face, a horrible idea coalescing in his mind. *You should feel guilty.* He searched for the emotion, for even an ember of remorse. Instead, survival instincts were pushing him, telling him Amos would understand. Hell, he would probably get a kick out of it. The bastard had always had a twisted sense of humor.

He pushed the sleeve of Amos's tattered uniform up

to examine the forearm. With a careful movement, he set the limb down and then leaned over sideways, stretching to reach the thin plastic bowl the glop had been served in.

He tipped the foul-smelling slime onto the floor and then smashed the bowl down with shaking arms. The plastic cracked, but didn't shatter. It took a few snaps to break up the dinnerware and get himself a useable piece.

Stomach clenching, he straightened and turned back to the body, forcing himself not to look up at the face. He wrapped one hand around the upper forearm, just under the elbow, and started hacking.

With single-minded focus, he set about retrieving the length of alloy in the forearm. After a few minutes, he started sweating cold. Shivers spasmed through him every now and then, but he didn't pause in his task. The CSS guards could come back any second.

Time did that distorting thing again. When he at last sat back with the length of metal in his hand, minutes could have gone by, or it might have been hours. With a surge of icy satisfaction, he shuffled over to the wall and braced himself against the cement to climb to his feet. Breathing harsh over the pain, he maneuvered himself next to the door and let the frame prop him up. The room spun, so he closed his eyes and focused on the sure feel of the alloy rod in his hand.

The familiar clicking noise sounded in the door's lock. Kai snapped his eyes open and forced his head up, tightening his grip on the measly weapon. The door swung outward and a figure loomed.

Kai swung his body weight around, putting every single pound he had in the momentum behind his hand. He stabbed the rod into flesh and then slammed into the robed soldier. They both went down, Kai ramming the bar home as he came out on top.

A different hand grabbed his shoulder as a shout reverberated in the enclosed space. With a sharp wrench, Kai pulled the alloy free and launched up from his knees. Pain screamed through his bad leg, right up into his back with a near-paralyzing intensity. But it didn't stop him from shoving the bar into the neck of the other soldier.

He collapsed in a tangle with the second robed man. Drained, Kai rolled into the corner where the floor met the wall, waiting for one of the CSS guards to get up and end his wretched existence. His leg and lower back throbbed, while his brain sloshed around his skull with a sickening force.

Silence fell and nothing moved. He lifted his head and looked at the two unmoving CSS guards. Blood seeped from underneath both men and crept across the concrete floor toward him. With teeth clenched, Kai forced himself up and closer to the fallen pair. Had he killed them? He didn't care and couldn't muster the energy to check. Instead he yanked the alloy bar, slick with blood, from the second soldier's neck.

Now what? His thoughts were thick and sluggish. He hadn't considered he might bring down the guards so easily. The door creaked in the icy dungeon draft and he dragged his gaze up to the opening.

Clarity exploded into his mind hard enough to give him an aneurism.

Escape.

Kai wasn't going to sit there and wait for more guards to turn up. He'd probably still end up dead, but at least this way he'd go out with a fight, instead of dying in the tiny, bare cell that had been his only reality for too many months.

He dropped the bloody alloy rod and it clanged loudly on the concrete floor. Lowering himself beside the nearest soldier was almost as hard as getting upright. Trying to maneuver himself down while keeping his bad leg straight was awkward; one shift in the wrong direction and he'd end up flat on his back, immobile with pain.

Once he'd gotten down, he yanked at the soldier's robes. He didn't expect to find anything useful like an electromagnetic pulse gun or a three-phase stunner pistol; the CSS didn't believe in technology. However, he did find an old-fashioned semi-automatic pistol. It took him a second to find the mag release on the outdated weapon, and a check revealed there were seven bullets in reserve, plus one in the chamber. He secured the cartridge and then shuffled over to the other soldier. A quick search revealed a dull knife and nothing else. Obviously the prison guards didn't expect much resistance. Then again, the CSS weren't exactly the most reliably fitted-out army. The only reason they'd held out in the two-decade-long war had been through superior numbers and sheer tenacity.

He shoved the knife into his belt and tightened his grip around the semi. With a short puffed breath, he pushed himself up again, using the wall to steady himself.

The walk past the two dead soldiers and through the doorway seemed to take forever as he strained to hear over his panting breaths, to listen out for any more guards coming his way. There wouldn't be any monitors to avoid, considering the CSS shunned as much technology as they could, apart from the things they deemed necessary to fight their war, but in place of the cameras, there'd be more guards patrolling at frequent intervals.

He and Amos had amused themselves for a few weeks trying to work out the guards' pattern. Initially it had seemed somewhat random, but then Amos had realized it was periodically and purposely haphazard. There was a pattern in the apparent disorganization of the patrols. It had taken another few weeks after that, but they'd memorized the pattern and found the holes. He'd never dared hope the information would come in handy.

Just outside the doorway in the empty corridor, he paused, trying to remember when and which way the last patrol had gone. The hallway was almost darker than the cell had been. One torch sputtered in the cold draft farther down the passageway, sending weak snatches of light flickering along the rough concrete walls.

The prison had been built to double as a bunker. If the CSS needed to go to ground in this area, they simply killed the least valuable prisoners to make room for their soldiers. One such culling had happened a few months after he and Amos had been captured. He still couldn't decide if he'd been lucky the CSS had deemed him valuable enough to live, or if the ones who'd been mass-executed were the fortunate ones.

Voices echoed from somewhere to his right; impossible to tell if it was other prisoners or the patrolling guards he needed to avoid. He pushed off from the wall and limped along the corridor to the left, walking deeper into the shadows. Doors marched along either side of him, identical to the one he'd walked out of a few moments ago. Occasionally he'd hear snatches of whispered voices, and the commander within him stirred, reminding him that it was his people behind those doors, possibly even people from his ship, the *Valiant Knox*, people he should be helping set free. But he hadn't even considered grabbing the keys from the dead soldiers and, despite the guilt that heaped on top of the burn of leaving Amos behind, he wasn't going to turn around for the keys. Goddamn it, he could hardly hold on to his own survival, let alone take the responsibility for anyone else's.

Instead, he pushed himself onward, reaching out to touch his fingers to the damp wall as the darkness expanded. Was he heading deeper into the prison? He'd been half out of it from a brutal interrogation when they'd first brought him down here, and he had no idea which direction they'd come through the maze of corridors.

The wall he'd been tracing dropped from beneath his fingers. He groped for the adjacent side of the corner and carefully stepped around it. Something skittered across his feet—a rat or one of those fist-sized cockroaches that dwelled down here. He'd become acquainted with both over the months, and the sight of them didn't bother him anymore. He and Amos had tried to catch rats for extra food every now and then, but apparently even the rodents had been too smart to touch the slop served at each meal in the prison, and they hadn't found anything else to tempt the creatures with. As for the cockroaches, no matter how hungry he'd gotten, he couldn't stomach the thought of eating one of the giant bugs.

An eerie moaning sounded from somewhere ahead of him, making the hairs on the back of his neck prickle. Glancing up, he saw a square of light at the far end of the corridor.

Quickening his steps, he headed toward it, his breath catching in his chest at the largest slant of sunshine he'd seen in a long time. Halfway there, another corridor intersected into his, the echo of boot steps and low conversation heralding the end of his luck.

He paused at the corner and peeked around. A torch was set in the wall, blocking his vision, so he bent down a little. Four guards farther along the hallway— two carrying torches and two carrying semi-autos like him, which probably meant they had sixteen bullets to his eight. The only advantage he had was surprise. He could shoot the two with the guns first, taking out the immediate threat before moving on to the pair with the torches, but the sound of gunfire would bring every other guard within the prison walls. And the six bullets he might have left wouldn't go very far against a garrison worth of men.

He leaned back against the wall, closing his eyes as dizziness threatened his balance. His nutrient-starved body wasn't used to this much activity. Pain throbbed like a constant smolder in his bad leg, sporadically forking up into his back. Icy sweat trickled down his spine and dripped down his face, stinging his eyes, while his exhausted muscles clenched, not quite trembling, but on the verge of breaking into a weakened quaking.

His short-lived freedom was about to end.

Dull anger pushed at his exhaustion. At least he'd taken a couple of the bastards with him. He shifted, trying to lessen the pressure on his injured leg, and his foot knocked into something. He squinted down in the shadows to see some kind of bucket-sized tin can. Closer inspection revealed it had oil or fuel in it, probably whatever they used to keep the torches burning. Possibly not the best idea to leave it sitting so close to the torch just around the corner. One stray spark and—

He glanced back down and told himself he'd lost his mind. Solving his little patrolling-guards problem with an explosion was ridiculous. If a few gunshots would bring the rest of the prison guards down on him, then what would a detonation do? Plus, he didn't know how volatile the stuff was. He'd be just as likely to blow up himself or the entire goddamn prison complex. Except the fatalistic side of him didn't care. The pessimistic part of him that had already decided he was going to die here told him to light up and blow as many of the CSS bastards to hell as he possibly could.

He shoved the semi into the back of his pants, and then, with shaking hands, reached around and snatched the torch down from the wall. For a split second, he waited to see if any of the nearing guards had noticed his move, but they were laughing at something, their voices rising in an echoing ruckus.

Bending over, he picked up the half-full tin can and stepped far enough away from the corner to launch the container down the hallway. He finally got the guards' attention as it bounced, splattering the walls and the two guards at the front with dark, oily liquid. One of them brought their gun up, but Kai had already flung the torch.

As it landed, he didn't wait to see the results, but threw himself behind the corner opposite to where he'd been standing. His heart hammered hard enough against the inside of his chest to break his no doubt weakened ribs.

The guards shouted, their yells abruptly cut off by a deep whooshing sound. All of the air seemed to get sucked from around him, and he hunched down as a superheated wave blasted past him a second later. There hadn't been a deafening boom like he'd expected, and it seemed the actual flames had mostly burned themselves out at the source. A quick check over himself revealed nothing on fire.

The next breath of relief he took caught in the back of his throat, the air acidic with smoke and the scent of burning flesh. He coughed, yanking his shirt up over his face as he scrambled to his feet.

For a second, he'd forgotten about his damned leg. But the sudden movement and resulting lance of pain reminded him with sickening force as he lurched into the wall to stop from pitching over. But he didn't stop. Because somehow his luck was holding, and maybe the fire would distract the guards from noticing his escape.

At the end of the hallway, the square of sunlight turned out to be a barred window. The hallway ended in a T, the branching corridors running the perimeter of the prison, with more barred windows at regular intervals. A rusty siren echoed from somewhere outside, causing some of the other prisoners to start yelling.

With absolutely no clue where anything led, he turned left again. Halfway along this hallway, there was a square, squat container overflowing with he-didn't-want-to-know-what, sitting beneath a hatch marked WASTE.

By the time he reached the end of the corridor, his breath was sawing in and out of his lungs, drying the back of his throat. He paused at the corner and snatched a look around, cursing under his short breath as he saw another patrol of four. Worse, they were stationary for the moment, waiting for a second patrol to catch up with them. That would be eight coming his way once they started moving. He turned around, headed back the way he'd come, intending to see what the opposite end of the hallway presented.

However, as he passed the halfway point with the waste container, he hesitated. The hatch wasn't exactly big; a kid would manage down it easy enough. But an adult? It would be a tight fit around his shoulders, but then again, starvation had definitely slimmed him down. It was an unlocked, presumably unguarded, opening to the outside, and probably his best option.

Kai clambered awkwardly onto the side of the container, holding his breath against the revolting smell—worse than the usual dungeon scent constantly lacing the prison air. It took two attempts to get his injured leg up, and he swore at himself in growing frustration, knowing his time was running out. If not for the goddamn gimpy leg, he could have been gone from here by now, and not half-out-of-his-mind from pain.

At last, he got his legs positioned and then shuffled forward, getting his thighs and hips in until he was sitting on the edge like an oversized kid on a slide. Exhaling hard, he gripped the outer lip and propelled himself inward. His shoulders scraped the edges like he'd guessed, but he still slid down slowly. After an impossibly long few seconds, his feet hit nothing but air, the rest of his legs following.

Ah, hell. He hadn't considered what kind of drop might be between the end of the chute and wherever the waste ended up. But with nothing to grab onto, he couldn't do anything but keep sliding. His heart skipped a few rushed beats and then froze on him as he left the chute altogether. Sunlight blinded him, and a second later he landed with a *plop* into a pool of thick, chunky liquid. Luckily it wasn't deep, and he ended up sitting chest-deep.

If the smell of the container inside had been bad, then this was horrific. Outside, under the sun, whatever waste had been sent down here had ripened to an indescribable sinus-stripping foulness. He gagged and struggled through the slop. The decomposing torso and arm he pushed out of his way confirmed what he'd been hoping wasn't true. Shutting down his mind, he waded to the edge and clambered out of the muck.

He couldn't breathe without gagging on exhale, and he stumbled away from the refuse, almost tripping over a roll of barbed wire. He looked up, finding himself on the far side of the prison. He'd studied enough aerial photos of the CSS's Enlightening Camp to know the outside layout in his sleep. This side of the prison was inapproachable for someone trying to get in. A few feet beyond him, a waist-high razor-wire fence had been built on top of rock, which dropped off in a sheer face down to a fast-flowing river. Beyond that was thick forest for miles, which eventually ran into the battlefront.

He'd gotten this far, but the pain and physical exertion were taking their toll, plus a gut-clenching sickness had taken hold now that he was covered in the stench of rot. But instinct told him he had to keep going until he couldn't move any more, until death was the only freedom he'd find.

He stumbled toward the razor-wire fence, cutting up his hands as he went over it and not feeling a single slice. The rocks beyond were slippery with the wind-whipped spray coming up off the river.

He sat down on the edge, breathing the fresh dampness, and the darkness of the prison fell away from him, like shedding a robe. He'd done it, escaped into free air and warming sunshine.

A shout sounded from behind him, putting an abrupt end to his enjoyment of the brief escape. He looked over his shoulder and shaded his eyes against the morning sun. One of the guards on the roof had spotted him. Beyond that, black smoke billowed into the otherwise clear blue sky.

The guard rounded the roof toward him, and Kai turned back to the river, staring down past his feet to the rushing water below. He'd heard drowning wasn't a bad way to go. With only a slight push, he slid off the edge of the slippery rocks, plunging down into cold, blue-green oblivion.

Chapter Two

Sacha slapped a hand over her hip as her med-comm vibrated with furious insistence for the third time in as many minutes. Trying to keep her movements subtle, she pulled the device off her belt and looked at the screen.

Code Alpha-Red, med-lab Lima-One-Niner.

Doctor Macaulay glanced over at her as she pushed her chair back from the conference table and stood in a rush. Adrenaline spiked as her mind leaped ahead to what sort of scenario could have caused an alpha-red code, only reserved for when high-ranking personnel were in an extreme medical emergency. She could count on one hand the number of times she'd attended an alpha-red.

"Doctor Dalton?" Macaulay murmured just loud enough

for her to hear, but they'd still managed to catch the attention of everyone else in attendance. On the large screen at the front of the room, the surgeon stopped talking, interrupting the sub-space conference between the *Valiant Knox* and Earth.

"Is there a problem, Doctor?" The on-screen surgeon asked, his tone of voice indicating she better have stood up for a damn good reason, or she'd be slapped down to field medic assistant faster than a ship in hyper-cruise.

"Yes, actually." She cast a quick look around the half a dozen other doctors sitting at the table. "Has anyone else got their med-comm on?"

Heads shook, along with a few shrugs.

"Med-comms were supposed to be off for the duration of the conference," the on-screen surgeon said in an ominous rumble.

Sacha flashed her med-comm at Macaulay, who dropped his mag-pen and straightened in his seat.

Before he could say anything, she sent him a stubborn frown and murmured, "You placate Doctor Uptight and I'll get on this. Switch your damn med-comm on and I'll page you if I need help."

Macaulay started to argue, but the on-screen surgeon trumped him by demanding an explanation. Sacha didn't wait around to see how that panned out, but hauled butt out of the conference room and down the short corridor from the medical offices to the remedial facilities. As she scooted through the quarantine air-lock doors, a group of nurses and doctors standing outside med-lab lima-one-niner marked her destination.

She paused to shove her hands in the sani-unit and then snapped on a pair of gloves.

"What have we got?" She elbowed the nearest nurse, who turned out to be one of her friends, Cassidy Willow.

"A prisoner of war just brought up from Ilari. A patrol found him three clicks from the CSS's Enlightening Camp."

"A POW? Then why the alpha-red code?" She shouldered her way past the medicos gathered in the corridor. "Who is it, Lieutenant Shaw or Officer Lourdes?"

"Neither."

That one word brought Sacha up short just before she reached the doorway.

She looked back at Cassidy. "Shaw and Lourdes are the only two POWs the CSS have."

Cassidy shook her head, eyes glinting with a curious mix of amazement and sadness. "It's Commander Yang."

Sacha's heart stopped. The damn organ totally flat-lined on her and for a second everything went black. A hand wrapped around her bicep and she shook her head, willing her vision to clear. She'd never fainted in her life, but Jesus had she come close then.

"Sacha, are you all right?"

As everything came back into sharp focus and her brain kicked into high-gear, she focused on Cassidy's concerned expression.

"I'm fine. What's Commander Yang's condition?"

Her friend let her arm go and moved back half a step, then turned to another nurse nearby and grabbed a datapad, her manner all business. Sacha grasped hold of that professionalism and forced herself to disconnect.

Cassidy ducked her head to read from the datapad. "Commander Yang is not conscious at the moment. He's suffering dehydration, malnutrition, avitaminosis, cirrhosis on his liver, and a malformed leg that was broken and healed without medical attention. There are other minor issues, but those are the main concerns right now."

Sacha took the datapad and scanned over the display, noting the commander's vitals and other important factors. "All right, the automated med system can start taking care of the internal problems, that's all fixable. But we'll have to take a look at his leg."

She handed the datapad off and steeled herself, locking down her emotions as she made her lead-filled legs carry her forward into the room. Two other nurses were there, assisting the three lower-level doctors swarming in controlled chaos around the commander's bed.

Sub-Doctor Archie Moore looked up, relief crossing his face when he spotted her approaching the bed. "Doctor Dalton, we've been paging you for—"

"I know, I'm sorry. I was in that Earth-link sub-space conference. You're lucky I flipped off the rules and still had my med-comm on. Where are we up to?"

Moore stepped back and Sacha got a clear view to the bed.

Kai. *Oh god.*

Shaggy black hair and a thick scruffy beard obscured most of his face. But what she could see of his features were battered, the skin a sickly gray. Scars he'd never had before puckered in white slashes. His body was lean, too thin, the loss of muscle mass obvious. All over, he was dirty, banged up, and in horrific shape. The broken leg was obvious in the shocking angle of his calf.

She clenched her fists, forcing the swelling tsunami of emotions down. The surge battered at her training, at every inch of practiced gloss she had. But she fought back the distress with the knowledge that unless she wanted to get tossed out to the waiting room, she could not react in any way, shape, or form to the horrible sight in front of her. If she so much as blinked wrong, they'd bring up Macaulay or Donavan to treat Kai and she wouldn't get a ring-in.

She only caught half of what Moore said as she dragged her attention back to him. But she trusted the medico staff on the *Valiant Knox*, knew they'd have a firm handle on this, especially considering it was their commander lying in that bed.

"Thanks, Moore. Now let's see about that broken leg." She skirted around to get a closer look at Kai's lower right calf. With a quick, assessing glimpse, she checked over the half a dozen or so machines hooked up to him. Some were simply monitoring, while others were repairing internal injuries and providing much-needed sustenance to his nutrient-starved body.

She bent down and touched his foot, searching for signs of vessel damage or indications the nerves might be compromised.

One of the machines let out a series of staccato beeps and she straightened, the alarm indicating Kai was regaining consciousness.

"Commander Yang, are you with me? You're back on the *Knox*, sir. We've got you in Doctor Dalton's med-lab." As Moore leaned over and flashed a light in front of the commander's eyes, Sacha straightened.

Kai rolled his head away from Moore's grip. The shadow of a familiar scowl that crossed his face made Sacha's heart spasm with a bittersweet elation. The urge to move closer to him tugged deep within her, but she made her feet stay right where they were.

Kai dragged a hand over his face, before blinking groggily and then widening his eyes. "Amos."

The word scraped out hoarse and he cleared his throat. No one in the med-lab moved or made a sound. Sacha held her breath as the tension in the room ratcheted up.

Kai swallowed. "Amos didn't make it."

It took a second for Sacha's mind to make sense of the words. *Sergeant Amos Claus.* He'd been down on Ilari with Kai when the two men had disappeared, assumed KIA.

Killed in action.

Those three words had sent her into a desolate nightmare, one that had just kept getting worse. Until today.

Moore moved first, breaking the thick atmosphere set into the air of the room.

"Commander Yang, tell me where you are. Do you know what year it is?" Moore tried to flash the penlight in his eyes again, but he swatted the sub-doctor away with a surprisingly agile movement.

"You just told me I'm back on the *Knox* and I'm guessing it's Twenty-Four-Thirty-Six." His voice might have been scratchy, but he sounded like the commander who'd fearlessly held the Ilari line these past five years. The same commander who could send a new recruit running with a single, well-aimed glare. The man she'd gotten trashed with on more than one occasion in the officers' lounge, laughing so hard at the way the poor newbies fell over themselves trying to please him. "But I don't know exactly how long I was in that prison."

"One year, four months, and three weeks." Sacha hadn't

meant to say that out loud, but the words tripped over her tongue before she could catch them. All of the doctors and nurses in the room paused to stare at her.

Great way to stay detached. She'd bet her next year's worth of paychecks no one else knew exactly how long ago Commander Yang had gone missing.

"Sacha?" If his voice had been hoarse before, now it came out so rough, the sound made her eyes sting. Or maybe it was the fact she'd never thought to hear him call her name ever again. She met his topaz-brown eyes and her heart pounded against the insides of her ribs with aching intensity.

She forced a smile and swallowed over the band of emotion choking her. "Hey there, Commander. You've caused a riot around here. Not every day a man returns from the dead."

His gaze sharpened on her. "Someone in personnel got it wrong, 'cause I sure as hell never died."

For a long moment she held his gaze, until a single drop of moisture gathered at the edge of his sooty black lashes and rolled slowly down the side of his face.

Her heart clenched and then ached. *God.* How much more of this could she take before she broke and gave into the impulse to sob all over him and thank the powers-that-be he'd come back to her alive after all this time?

With a small sniff and a damn large helping of determination, she forced her attention down to his mangled leg.

"Moore, we're going to have to re-break this leg before putting it in the bone-mending cylinder. Get me a shot of hyproxen. That'll put him out cold and keep the pain manageable."

"No!" Kai reared up, jerking the various cords attached

to him. Moore and a male nurse caught his shoulders and tried to urge him back.

Anger and indignation roared through her at the sight. Sacha hip-and-shouldered the male nurse out of the way. Couldn't they see how panicked Kai was? After everything he'd been through, horrors that she didn't even want to begin to imagine, the two men getting physical with him would only make things worse.

She leaned over and shoved Moore back a step, before catching Kai's face, his beard scratchy and springy beneath her palms.

"Kai. *Kai*, look at me."

His thrashing subsided, but his breath heaved in and out of his chest as his wild topaz gaze clashed with hers.

When she had his attention focused solely on her, a relieved breath rushed out of her. "It's all right. Just tell me what you want and we'll deal."

The out-of-control alarm eased from his expression and he relaxed back against the pillows. "No drugs. *Please*, don't knock me out."

Jesus, Mary and Joseph. What had the CSS done to him?

She swallowed and let her hands slip down from his face. "Okay, we won't put you under. We'll just give you something for the pain."

"*No*. I can't—I won't—" He started shaking, his whole body wracking with deep shudders.

Sacha clamped a hand on his shoulder. "It's all right. We won't do anything you don't want us to do."

She couldn't do anything about the rusty tenor of her voice, betraying the emotions ripping her up inside. But anyone who saw their commander now would no doubt have trouble staying detached in the face of this reality.

To steady herself, she took a long breath. "But we're going to have to re-break your leg. It's not going to be pretty."

He clenched his jaw and dropped his head back to stare at the ceiling. "I don't care. Just do it and don't give me anything."

Sacha glanced over at Moore, who appeared pale and more than a little shaken. But they were the ones who had to be strong, who had to pull the commander back together and then hold him up until he could stand on his own.

She steeled her spine and moved back to the end of the bed. "You heard the commander. Let's get this done and then leave the man to rest."

Moore and the male nurse joined her and she quickly instructed them where to hold and how she wanted to proceed. They wouldn't need to use any instruments. Because of Kai's malnutrition and the angle of the bone, she could tell it was a simple snap away from being in the right place. Once she freed and re-aligned the bone, the bone-mending cylinder—or BMC—would heal the injury completely within twenty-four hours.

When she was sure everyone had gotten on board with the game plan, she wrapped a hand around the ankle and lower calf. She didn't have to do much, just twist in counteraction to Moore.

Sacha glanced up and caught Kai's glinting stare.

"Are you sure you want to do this without pain meds?" Her voice wavered like an intern on her first gory case.

He gave a single jerk of his head, and then returned to staring at the ceiling. His large hands wrapped around the rails of the bed, banged-up knuckles showing white with the pressure of his hold.

Preparing herself, Sacha looked from Moore to the male nurse. They had to get this right the first time.

"On three, gentlemen. One…two…three!"

She and Moore wrenched in opposite directions and a sickening, dull crack echoed a split second before Kai roared. The shout sounded near animalistic, with the kind of painful intensity that made the hairs on the back of her neck prickle. Kai went rigid all over for a long moment and then collapsed into a boneless heap.

"The commander is unconscious again," the male nurse reported after a brief check.

She helped Moore set the bone to where it should be and then braced both of her hands against the edge of the bed, her limbs feeling like jelly. One of the other sub-doctors brought the BMC over and with Moore's help, she positioned it over the damaged calf.

"Good work, Doctor Dalton." Someone touched her briefly on the shoulder. Her peripheral senses were aware of people moving around her, but for a few moments she could only lean against the bed and stare at the man she'd mourned for almost a year and a half.

With a ragged breath she straightened, needing some time and space to decompress, to unwind and get used to the fact that Commander Kai Yang was alive and for the most part, okay.

"Comm me when he wakes up, and let me know if anything changes," she instructed no one in particular. But the sub-doctors and nurses around her all returned agreements.

She turned and maneuvered past all the medical staff, going against the tide to head back toward the quarantine air-lock doors that separated the med-facilities from the rest of the ship.

The doors whooshed open and Doctor Macaulay rushed through, along with several other doctors who still should have been in the conference with him.

Macaulay grabbed her shoulder. "Is it true? Have they got Commander Yang in there?"

Mustering a nod, she called on the thin wire of professional detachment keeping her together. "The commander is in bad shape, but considering where he's been the past year and a half, it could have been worse. He's not conscious, but he was awake and lucid for a little while."

A murmur rippled between the other doctors as Macaulay muttered a curse.

She gently pulled out of his hold. "If you'll excuse me, Commander Emmanuel and Captain Phillip will be waiting to hear some details, I need to go debrief them."

He stepped back and ran a hand through his hair. "Of course. Go, I'll keep an eye on things here until you get back."

She nodded a reply and then continued through the airlock and out past offices and conference rooms. When she reached the transit-porter—which went between levels of the ship or from one end to the other—instead of going up to the command center, she went down to crew deck.

At this time of day, the ship's level of crew housing was pretty much deserted. Which suited her just fine. She didn't have to wear her Doctor Dalton mask as she took the short walk from the lift to her quarters.

The door slid silently open from a personalized remote sensor as she got closer. Inside, she only made it as far as the couch in the small living area before her legs gave out and she collapsed heavily on the cushions. Tears came hard and fast. And then a sob clenched her chest. She hiccupped for air and got attacked by another round of soul-deep sobbing, grief welling up from where she'd shoved it so she wouldn't have to deal.

First Kai, her oldest friend, had been listed KIA. And then not even six months later, Elliot had been killed going in hot over Ilari lines, trying to provide air backup for the men caught on the ground. How many times had she had the "stupid risks" argument with her husband? And just as she'd feared, he'd been taken down trying something that most people would have deemed as insurmountable odds.

At least she'd been able to put Elliot to rest and send him back to his parents for a memorial service. There'd never been a body for Kai's funeral. Just an empty spot in a military graveyard where others considered KIA had also been laid to rest.

A hysterical laugh bubbled up under her tears. They'd had a full five-star military *funeral* for Kai, and he'd been alive all along. Wait until he heard about that.

Her gaze crept over to the display case in the corner of the room, where two yellow-ribbon, bronze medals sat under soft lights in the topmost shelf.

One for Elliot. And one for Kai.

For honor, bravery, and great sacrifice in the line of duty... The words Commander Emmanuel had spoken on the two separate days she'd gone up to accept those medals.

Bone-deep weariness stole over her and she closed her eyes on a long sigh. She'd just rest a minute, pull her crap together, and then she'd get her butt up to the command center where Kai's replacement commander would be waiting for a report on the patient.

Chapter Three

Kai shifted his hips, not able to go far with the various cords attached to him and BMC enclosing his damaged leg.

After spending the past year and a half with a slab of concrete for a bed, the fact that the pillows behind him were so damn uncomfortable seemed ridiculous. His bad leg burned, itched, and ached all at the same time while the cylinder sped up the body's natural bone-knitting process.

And while he was bitching, the bright sterile lights in the room made his eyes twitch and a slice of pain shoot right through the middle of his skull after being in semi-darkness for so long. Everything around him had a soft blur. One of the sub-doctors had mentioned something about optical atrophy, which would apparently get repaired once his body's functions were back on track.

The door to his room stood open, and even though the clock near his bed read oh-two-hundred ship-time, not five minutes would go by without at least one medico ducking in to check something or other. Lucky he didn't feel like sleeping, or all the hustle would have kept him wide awake.

His surroundings had an edge of surrealism to them. For so long, the only people he'd seen were Amos and the robed CS Soldiers. In the past few hours, all the faces of the people who'd been in and out of his room had fritzed his brain. The only clear face he had in his mind belonged to Sacha in those hazy few minutes before she'd gone and re-broken his goddamn leg.

His whole body clenched at the memory of the wrenching pain, so he shut down that line of thinking.

Sacha had left while he'd been out of it and hadn't returned. Doctor Macaulay had taken her place in ordering the other doctors and nurses around. Before Kai had been captured by CSS, Macaulay had always rubbed him the wrong way. And now he had the guy in charge of his care.

Where the heck was Sacha?

A few times he'd almost asked the nurses shuffling in and out, but in truth, he didn't want to know the answer. He'd seen the stark emotions playing across her face when they'd taken that long second to really look at each other. She'd probably been busted off his case because she was too emotionally involved with the patient.

His mind dragged up the memory of the first day he'd met her, when he'd been sixteen and she'd been thirteen, and they'd been allocated the same class at pre-military school. She'd been so smart, they'd put her up a couple of grades. Some of the other kids had made fun of her, but he'd always thought she was interesting. Though they hadn't been very close from the start, they'd had the same group of friends. Sacha had opted to go into medicine, while he'd put in for active duty and, by chance, they'd both been assigned to the *Valiant Knox* in their early twenties.

Sacha had always just been there. She'd met Elliot within a year of starting service on the *Knox* and Kai had been concentrating on moving up the ranks. All right, so occasionally over the years he'd looked at her and wondered *what if*. But he was truly happy she had Elliot and was content.

Still, when he heard her voice earlier, when he looked over and caught a glimpse of that bronze-spun hair and smoky blue gaze, his heart had gone into freefall. There'd been days in that CSS cell when the only thing he'd wanted was to see her again. Her memory had stayed with him a lot longer than anything else of his former life. And too many nights he'd dreamed of her, the images so vivid he'd woken up with an aching chest and moisture stinging his eyes.

A nurse strode into the room carrying a tray, an easy smile lighting up her face.

"Commander Yang, Doctor Macaulay has decided you're well enough to eat, so I've brought you some multi-jelly." She walked over and set the tray on a hover table before positioning it in front of him. The nutritional multi-supplement jelly gleamed in a rainbow of colors under the lights above him. "We've got watermelon flavor, green apple, mixed berry, or orange. Eat whatever you feel like, but the more you get down, the quicker you'll recover."

He reached down and wrapped a hand around one of the spoons. The nurse fussed and hovered for a few more moments until he sent her a commander-esque glare. After that she cleared the room in a nano-second flat. Sighing, he dropped his gaze to the rainbow assortment of jelly. The Commander Yang everyone else knew had ceased to exist in the dim, squalid cell down on Ilari. He had no damned idea who they'd brought back to the *Knox*. Yet everyone still jumped if he scowled at them the right way.

The door whooshed and he looked up from his poor excuse for a dead-watch meal to see Sacha standing in front of the closed door, hands in her pockets, expression unreadable.

His heart palpitated, words failing him at the profound relief her simple presence brought him.

"So Macaulay deemed you fit for jelly, huh?" She moved forward, coming over to casually hike her butt up onto the bed near his left thigh. "Yum, watermelon. Do you mind? I forgot to have dinner. And lunch as well, I think."

She grabbed one of the spare spoons and then popped the top off the pink-colored jelly.

"I'm sure Elliot isn't happy about you skipping meals. He's always complaining you're too skinny." The words were rough and awkward. He wasn't used to normal conversation that didn't involve torture, or imprisonment, or the damn CS Soldiers.

Sacha's eyes darkened to the color of bruised storm clouds as she regarded him for a brief moment, before returning her attention to scooping the jelly.

"Elliot's dead. He got shot down over Ilari lines about a year ago."

The words were even and emotionless, but he still caught the utter tragic undertone. Or maybe he imagined it. Either way, the fact that her husband had died not long after the CSS had captured him eroded his soul like acid. How had she coped, after losing them both?

He knew he should have been just as devastated by this news. Elliot had been one of his closest friends; he'd been the best man at their wedding five years ago. But after Amos, *after everything*, it seemed his body had run out of grief to expend.

"I'm sorry." He clenched his fist around the dull edges of the spoon. Those two words didn't even begin to cover the collision of emotions inside him.

"Don't be. You knew Elliot as well as I did. He knew the risks, yet he took them anyway. I think I'd known for a while it was just a matter of time before that day came. After you—" She paused and swallowed, then took a short breath. "When you went missing, he just got more reckless. It didn't matter what anyone said to him, didn't matter how much I loved him. He was determined to go out there and make a difference like a fricking one-man army."

Her words were tough, but he could see the shadows around her she'd never had before. Kai stared down at the three other jellies on the tray and then slowly picked up the orange one. "Elliot was a dick. With you waiting for him to come home, it made his risks even more idiotic."

He glanced up to catch the misty smile she sent him before she scooped up some more of the pink watermelon conserve. She held out the spoon toward him.

"You want some? Watermelon is the best. Everyone always steals it out of the cool-store whenever supplies come in. You must be an extra special patient if someone scrounged one up for you."

His lips twitched and astonishment burst through him. She made him want to *smile*. He couldn't even remember the last time his mouth had moved in an upward direction.

"You finish it off. I'll stick with orange."

A sharp rapping on the door drew his attention. He

glanced over, but Sacha didn't turn from where she had her back to the doorway, sitting on the bed.

Doctor Macaulay knocked on the pane again, his expression landing somewhere between indignant and pissed off.

"Sacha, Macaulay's at the door, and he doesn't look too impressed."

She shrugged, but didn't look up from finishing off her substitute meal, her actions telling him she didn't give a crap about Doctor Douche out in the corridor.

"I locked the door after I came in and secured it with my personal codes so no one else could enter." She lifted her gaze to him. The familiar mischievous glint in her eyes made him feel lighter, took him back to easier, happier times. Any prank they'd ever pulled had always started off when Sacha got that gleam in her smoky eyes. She'd never admit it, but she'd instigated more than her fair share of the trouble they'd found when they'd been younger.

At another round of furious banging, she sighed long and loud, and then turned to send Macaulay a mocking salute. Doctor Douche glared with annoyance while his face turned an interesting shade of red, and then he shoved off from the door to disappear from sight.

This time, when the foreign urge to grin hit him, he didn't resist, letting the expression tug at face muscles that hadn't been used in a while.

She turned to him once more and dropped the empty container on the tray. "I bet they haven't left you alone for more than five minutes at a time since you came in. I thought you could use a break."

"Thanks. The past few hours have been a tornado of

unending people." He reached up to scratch his jaw under the thick scruffy beard.

She tilted her head and regarded him with a thoughtful expression. "Now that you're on the way to healing, how about we start getting you cleaned up?"

He smoothed over the section of beard he'd been scratching at. The idea hadn't even occurred to him; he'd been shaggy and covered in whiskers for so long, he'd forgotten *not* having them was an option.

"What's wrong? Don't you like a man who can pull off a full beard and still strike fear into the hearts of his subordinates?" It was something his old self would have said with ease. After the words left his mouth, they made him feel like a fraud.

But Sacha didn't seem to notice anything amiss. She sent him a droll look, hopped off the bed and walked over to the various machines above his head.

With agile movements, she had the equipment off-line and all the cords disconnected in a matter of seconds.

"Are you sure that's a good idea? Macaulay said I needed over twenty-four hours of treatment." Though, he felt a hundred times better already. Various aches and pains he'd gotten used to living with had disappeared. Even the constant, subtle nausea that'd plagued him had gone, leaving him with the astounding sensation of being hungry.

Sacha glared at him as she leaned over to flick electrodes off his chest.

"Technically you're my patient, so you can take whatever Macaulay said and vacuum it out the nearest hatch. At this point you've come far enough in the healing process that being off the machines for half an hour won't make a difference. Though, your leg will probably ache some."

"And what are you going to do with me while I'm not plugged in?" With her leaning so close to him, when he breathed, all he smelled, all he tasted, was the familiar acacia and summer scent of her, overlaid by the med-lab's sanitizer.

After she'd flipped the last electrode free, she glanced up at him and the sight of her so close brought a rush of warm, euphoric sensation. His body buzzed to life, long-dormant sensations rushing through the blood in his veins. He got hot all over, her nearness sparking off a primal and darkly instinctive reaction within him.

"I'm taking you to the wash facilities over there"— she nodded toward the far corner where a drain in the floor sat under a gleaming steel shower nozzle—"and doing something about this caveman look you're rocking."

She straightened and then moved down to slide the BMC off his leg. The absence of tingling, itching heat helped him breathe a little easier, though a dull ache throbbed through the limb. A damn side better than the excruciating pain he'd endured ever since the bone had been broken.

Once he got free of all the bits and pieces, he shuffled his ass forward and swung his legs off the side of the bed with Sacha bracing a hand against his shoulder to keep him steady. But she needn't have bothered. Though an underlying sensation of fatigue and weariness dragged at him, overall he felt pretty good.

She took his elbow as he straightened to his feet and put his full weight on his bad leg. He could stand upright and not have to endure sparks of shooting pain spasming up into his back. *Thank the damn good Lord.*

Kai took a confident step, ignoring the spin of exhausted

dizziness through his head. Tired he could deal with. It was a far cry from half-dead. But Sacha set herself against him to support his weight as they walked slowly toward the wash facilities in the corner.

He clenched his jaw over the urge to snap at her. He could have walked just fine; he wasn't a damn invalid. But the feel of her soft curves pressed along the length of his side made him feel good in a way he hadn't for a long, long time. So he swallowed the words and concentrated on getting to the bench seat on the wall, under the shower nozzle.

Once he'd sat down, Sacha grabbed a remote from a nearby trolley, stuffed to overflowing with medical paraphernalia. He watched as one button lowered a screen over the pane in the door, giving the room total privacy, while another button made an opaque divider slide out and section off the wash facilities into a stall. With one last button, a stream of warm water whooshed out of the shower nozzle, causing steam to start frothing into the air.

While she busied herself with something else on the trolley, he leaned forward and stuck his head under the gentle jet of water. *Oh man*, nothing had ever felt so good. He sluiced his hair from his eyes and groaned as warm water trickled down his neck and over his bare chest.

The pajama-type pants he'd been given earlier started getting soaked. More than anything, he wanted to strip off and stand under the spray, letting it cover him all over. He looked at Sacha, who was setting out a row of tools on a tray. *Hmm*. She didn't look like she planned on going anywhere in the next few minutes.

So did he stay in his sopping pants, or get naked in front of her? She was a doctor, she'd seen it all before. But she was also his oldest friend and she hadn't seen all of *him* before. Actually. Scrap that. She had seen all of him before. When they'd gone skinny-dipping with a couple of other friends one sultry midnight on a holiday resort planet years ago.

But this was different. Closed together in the small wash facilities, it seemed more intimate.

Sacha turned to him with a pair of scissors in her hand. "What do you want to start on first, the beard or hair?"

He cleared his throat, a heated, humming awareness of her as a woman setting him on edge as she took two steps to close the distance between them. Jesus. He'd escaped from hell a little over twelve hours ago…yet here he sat with his blood pumping hard through his body as his thoughts started straying into sex-territory and his cock stirred in a way that told him just how alive he was.

Ignore it.

"Whichever you want."

She tilted her head, biting her lip between her teeth with a thoughtful expression. "I'm going to opt for the hair first. Okay, keep in mind, I'm not a hairdresser, but I'm sure I can neaten you to the point of respectability."

A deep sigh escaped him as she touched his hair, causing a ripple of sensation along his spine. "Whatever you do will be fine."

As her hand stroked through the tangles, Kai closed his eyes and let his head drop forward, relaxing under her touch in a way he hadn't been able to do since the day the CSS had nabbed him.

The warmth from the billowing steam and rhythmic *snip-snip* while Sacha worked lulled him and he let his mind drift into comfortable nothingness. The profound relief of being able to do something so simple hammered him, making his chest ache. With every slight tug of his hair, every time her nails scraped lightly over his scalp, small electrified tingles shot through his veins, yet the repetitive movements soothed him into a tranquil state.

The steam enhanced the acacia-summer scent of her skin until every breath he took was infused with her. Their earlier life together drifted through his mind, memories and moments he'd all but forgotten. *Friends*. He'd thought that's all they ever were, but the pounding in his chest told him a different story.

"I'm done with your hair. Can you lift your head so I can tackle the beard?"

Her words roused him from the light trance he'd fallen into. He caught the bemused expression on her face when he looked up and met her gaze.

"Were you sleeping, Commander?"

"So what if I was? It's almost oh-two-thirty and none of your people have let me shut my eyes for a minute."

"Ouch. Point taken, *sir*." She crouched down in front of him, leaning against his left thigh, and then set the scissors to his thick beard.

As she methodically cut away the long whiskers, he watched her face. His heart skipped a couple of beats, hiccupping behind his ribs. *God*, she'd always been so adorable when she concentrated hard. His fingers itched to trace the smoothness of her skin.

Neither of them spoke as she cut away what she could and then lathered up his face with shaving cream. Her fingers soothed and massaged flesh that had only known pain for too long. The constant hissing of the shower saved the silence from getting too loud and created an extra layer to the cocooning sensation of being in the stall.

Sacha paused with the razor in her hand and he looked down to catch her smoky gaze. The steam had pinked her skin, giving her a damp, healthy glow. Her clothes were rumpled and splotched with water. Tendrils of bronze-spun hair had started curling at her neck and near her temples. He clenched his fist on the edge of the bench seat as his body tightened up all over, blood rushing through his limbs in a burning surge. *Christ.* This time he couldn't ignore the sensations she roused within him. What an epically bad time to be hit with a massive surge of lust. He'd almost forgotten what that felt like…

"Something wrong?" His voice came out scratchy, so he cleared his throat.

"I was just wondering if you wanted to do this part yourself. Honestly, I haven't got the first clue about shaving a guy. The best experience I've got is when we shave people for surgery and even then they're unconscious…" A small, awkward smile kicked up her lips and the sight overloaded his brain. Images of hauling her into his lap and losing himself in her sweetness jammed up his mind until he couldn't think of anything else.

With ruthless will, he forced the fantasy away. She was married to one of his closest friends. *No.* Not married anymore. Goddamn Elliot had gotten himself killed. But she wasn't here as his friend, she was acting as his doctor. He dampened the raging impulses and made his mind focus on the mundane task of shaving.

"Didn't you ever do this for Elliot?"

She dropped her gaze to the razor in her hand. "No, I

guess I never thought about wanting to and he never asked. It was just one of a whole mess of things we never did with each other."

Damned if the idea of doing something with her that she'd never shared with her husband didn't strike him low in the guts and send the heat surging harder.

You're a bastard, Kai. She was probably still mourning. Not to mention she'd thought him dead for over a year. If there was a medal on inappropriate times and places for getting jacked up over a woman, he'd just taken the grand prize.

But whatever small shred of honor he had over the improper feelings didn't stop him from opening his mouth. "I'd like it if you finished."

She stared at him for a long moment and for half a second he thought she'd refuse. But then she leaned closer to him. When her soft fingers touched his chin, a shudder ripped down his spine, turning his insides to mush.

He closed his eyes as she started carefully shaving off the trimmed whiskers, because if he looked at her any longer, the thin threads of his control would snap and he'd end up doing something they'd both regret. *Doctor and friend,* he repeated again and again. Nothing else to it.

Maybe he could blame the surge of hot desire over the fact he'd been in prison with only men for company the past year and a half. Or the need to reaffirm he was alive by doing something base that came natural to all human beings. Whatever the reason, he still had enough brains to know acting on the carnal longing wouldn't help either of them.

Chapter Four

Sacha made herself focus on the patch of skin she was shaving, not giving in to the impulse to look at Kai's face, gradually revealed under her ministrations. Her gaze strayed upward and a flutter started in her stomach.

Damn it. So much for not looking.

Without the thick covering of hair, and despite a new leanness to his physique, Kai was just as masculine and gorgeous as he'd always been. His thick, sooty lashes hid his topaz eyes and his now-trimmed midnight-black hair framed the strong angles of his face.

She couldn't quite draw a full breath in the thick steam of the shower, making her heartbeat irregular. Or maybe her erratic pulse had something to do with the fact she was touching a man she'd thought dead for the past year and a half. Oh, and her rampaging hormones had some serious ideas about what she should be doing with a half naked, dripping, damn sexy man in the shower.

Get a grip, woman.

Kai had just come out of hell. He no doubt had a million other more important things on his mind. And even if she'd always felt a spark of something with him, they'd been friends for sixteen years. Crossing the line to anything else just wouldn't happen.

She groped in her mind for some professional detachment, but couldn't find even a speck. All right, new game plan. Finish shaving him as quick as possible and get the hell out of the shower.

With smooth, swift strokes, she managed to concentrate on the task well enough to get it done and not nick his skin. He turned his head this way and that at her murmured commands, but he didn't open his eyes. Part of her was relieved over that; it made the task less intense without him watching her.

It also made it easier for her forbidden thoughts to run rampant, because without him staring at her, she didn't need to hide her thoughts as she let her gaze roam over the new leanness of his chest. While he had definitely lost the bulkier muscles he'd once had, his physique still appeared to be healthy enough. The CSS might not have fed him properly, but at least they hadn't starved him into a walking skeleton. A flush of heat bloomed within her that had nothing to do with the steam billowing around them.

She stood in a rush once she'd scraped the last of his whiskers away. "There, all done. I'll give you a few minutes of privacy to finish washing up."

He blinked open his eyes and stared up at her. The sparking gleam in his golden gaze made her lungs constrict. Water dripped from his now-short hair, down the strong column of his throat and over the compact muscles of his chest. She clenched her fists so hard, fingernails bit into her palms.

Leaving… Leaving right now.

She spun away from him and reached for the screen latch.

"Wait."

Though he hadn't touched her and the word had been a quiet murmur, she jolted to a stop as though he'd physically yanked her back. With breath held, she didn't dare move a muscle, unsure of what she might do if she let go of what little sanity she had left.

A warm, heavy hand landed on her shoulder and at the slight pressure, she found herself turning to face him.

"I haven't had a shower since I got captured. I need to be clean all over." He pressed his lips together, a muscle flexing in his jaw as he took a deep breath. "Please, help me?"

Holy hell. Commander Yang actually asking for help. No one would believe it if she ever told them. The commander she could deny, but her oldest friend, Kai, asking…? Well, that she could never say no to, despite her mind telling her it was a bad, *bad* idea. She nodded, groping for her professional mask, but unable to find it. Instead she felt her cheeks warming as her imagination supplied her with the picture of Kai stripping out of the PJ pants. At least with all of the steam, she could blame her flushed face on that.

He let out a relieved-sounding breath and limped back to the seat. "I need to scrub the grime of that place off every inch."

When he sat back down and glanced up at her, she saw the shadows of lingering horror in his eyes and her heart squeezed painfully. *Oh, Kai.* She'd been so wrapped up in her own hormones, and there he sat, needing her help.

With renewed determination to help him forget, she went to the trolley and grabbed a washcloth and a bottle of liquid soap. By the time she turned back to him, he had shifted enough to take off his pants. They lay in a sodden heap by his feet. He had his head tilted back against the tiled wall, his eyes closed. No doubt he was getting tired. She needed to get him into bed and hooked back up so he could finish his recovery.

She kicked the pants out of the way and then crouched in front of him, keeping her eyes on his feet, because right then, she couldn't consider all the places she would have to wash him without her heart going into palpitations.

With a gentle touch, she cleaned and rinsed his feet, ankles and calves, right up to his knees. Every so often he'd shift, or make a slight noise, or she'd look up to find an expression of fierce concentration on his face, though he kept his eyes closed. Was his bad leg hurting? She didn't dare pause to ask.

She gentled her touch even more, lightly massaging as she lathered the soap, and then passing long, slow strokes over his skin as she washed the suds away, revealing clean, though pale, flesh. As she got higher, past his knees to the thick muscles of his thigh, she determinedly kept her gaze attached to her hand. But she couldn't do anything about the increasing pound of her heart, or the shortening of her breath. No matter how she tried to hold onto her professional morals, where Kai was concerned, the line blurred too easily, and she was definitely enjoying this far more than she had any right to.

She stood, her thighs burning slightly from crouching for so long. "Do you think you'll be able to stand long enough for me to do the rest of you?"

He stood and turned his back to her, not meeting her gaze. Did he feel uncomfortable about having her do this for him? She swallowed and studied the muscled expanse of his back. Adding more soap and water to the cloth, she started at his shoulders and rubbed down over the blades, along his spine, and into his lower back. She couldn't have said how much time passed. Maybe it was a few minutes, maybe it was much longer, she had become so absorbed in running the cloth over his firm skin.

"All done. Turn around and I'll finish up for you." Her voice came out a little husky, and she cleared her throat as she stepped back so he could turn toward her. When he faced her, she caught his eyes, and a fire burned in their depths. Automatically, she reached up to feel his skin for a fever, but he caught her wrist before she made contact.

With a slow movement, he shifted forward until he towered above her, never taking his smoldering gaze from hers. Comprehension dawned and brought a tingling surge of sparkling elation from the depths of her bruised heart. She swallowed and tried to take a step back, but he simply matched her pace, keeping them too close together.

Rest. Medication. Sleep. Those were the things he needed to heal. She took another step away from him, but the wall came up against her back and he kept coming until she was trapped.

Electrifying heat rushed through her as his damp body came up against hers. Her fingers went limp and the washcloth dropped from her hand to land with a *splat* on the tiles.

"Kai—" She couldn't get the word out past a whisper, but it wouldn't have mattered what she said in that moment—

she could see he'd gone far beyond any sense of reasoning. And more than anything, she wanted to go there with him.

Rational thought abandoned her as she surged up, winding an arm around his neck and closing her mouth over his. She shocked herself, because she hadn't realized what she was going to do until she was already doing it. Kai groaned, the sound guttural, rising from deep within his chest, and he wrapped both his arms around her as he shoved her up against the wall.

Her head spun, and every muscle in her body clenched in a heated, rippling wave, whipping up a twisting storm of rapture within her. She couldn't grab onto any one thought clearly with the way Kai's mouth melded against hers, his tongue crossing her lips and making her shudder all the way to her toes.

He devoured her like a starving man, the kiss so carnal and full of desperate yearning she felt it in every cell of her body, like ice meeting flame and erupting into steam.

And then the truth of the situation struck her right in the middle of the chest and she had to pull away from him to gulp in a mouthful of air.

He *had* been starved, for companionship, for basic human interaction and compassion. As his doctor and friend, kissing him was about the worst thing she could do; the psychological fallout could be horrible for both of them.

"Kai, you've been through a lot, I'm sorry, I shouldn't have—"

He grinned at her and stepped back into the spray of the shower. With that spark in his gaze, he looked more like his old self. And the smile he sent her was the one he always used when he thought she was talking crap. Maybe kissing hadn't been all bad? It certainly hadn't been for her.

She found herself taking a step toward him as her attention dropped down his body. He bent to pick up the washcloth and ran it across himself, leaving soapy trails over the lean, sculpted muscles of his chest. Her gaze slid farther down and stopped at the junction of his thighs. She flushed hot at the sight of his erection and automatically spun to put him at her back as though she were some flighty schoolgirl.

"Do you need any more help?" She squeezed her eyes shut. *Idiot. Now what are you going to do if he says yes? Refuse?*

"No, I'm suddenly feeling much cleaner." The tenor of his words shivered down her spine and all she could think of was stripping out of her own clothes and joining him under the warm spray. Except she couldn't be that selfish. No matter how much she might want him—to run her hands over every inch of his body if only to confirm that he was real and had actually come back to her—he needed her as a doctor more than he needed a friend or anything else right now.

Get your butt out of here, woman!

With a short fumble over the latch on the rim of the screen, she managed to get out of the stall and not look at him and his naked body of dripping enticement again.

"When you want to turn the water off, just press the blue button on the remote. And yell if you need anything," she called out over the rush of water.

He murmured an agreement. With a shake of her head, Sacha walked over to sit on the bed. She smoothed her water-splotched, steam-rumpled shirt and then pulled a bag of candy-coated chocolate out of her pocket. Oh boy, did she need some sugar.

Through the opaque screen, she could just make out the silhouette of Kai as he stood under the shower nozzle. A flush of searing heat burned through her as she remembered the feel of his hard body up against her, so she got up and made herself sit on the other side of the bed, with her back to the stall. Determinedly keeping her mind off what was going on behind her, she ate the chocolates, four or five at a time, until she'd finished the bag. The water shut off as she tossed the wrapper in the trash.

"There are towels and clean pajamas on that trolley." She busied herself bashing the pillows on the bed into shape with more force than necessary and then pulled at the sheets sharp enough to tear them.

"Thanks, I found them."

A few moments later, the screen hummed its way back into the wall recess, revealing Kai in a new set of PJ bottoms, scrubbing a towel over his damp hair. He dropped the cloth and then limped forward, holding a hand out to ward her off when she started over to help him. He shot her a stubborn look and made his own way over to the bed. Must be feeling better if he was getting his old I'll-drop-before-I-let-anyone-help-me attitude back again.

She crossed her arms and watched as he stiffly climbed onto the bed and settled himself against the pillows. He sent her a smug grin and picked up the orange jelly he hadn't touched before. For the first time since she'd walked into this room and seen him, he really did seem more like his old self and something tight in her chest released and unwound.

"Well then, if you don't need me, I guess I'll go home and get some sleep. You know I'm not even on-shift tonight, I just came in to make sure you were doing okay."

"How considerate of you, Doctor Dalton." He woofed down the jelly and gave her a look that said he saw right through her guilt trip.

She couldn't help but smile, since she felt lighthearted for the first time in too long, like she could actually look forward to tomorrow. Kai abandoned the empty jelly cup and patted the edge of the bed before he picked up the mixed berry one.

With a silent sigh, she walked over to join him.

He shot her a brief, guarded look. "Tell me what else I've missed. I heard Commander Emmanuel took over my post?"

"Are you sure you're ready to hear it all? Maybe you should get some sleep."

He shrugged one shoulder. "I won't be able to sleep if I'm lying here wondering what happened while I was out of commission. Just give me the footnotes version."

As he finished off the rest of the multi-jelly on the tray, she glossed through a year and a half worth of politics, advances in the war against the CS Soldiers, and the more personal gossip that'd happened onboard the *Knox*. He listened with a quiet intensity, not asking any questions or making any comments.

"And that's about it, really," she said as way of finishing.

Kai sank back against the pillows, gazing off toward the doorway still shuttered with the privacy screen. She got the feeling he wasn't seeing anything, but instead trying to absorb everything she'd told him.

"The only question now is, where do I belong?"

Her heart plummeted at the desolate edge to his voice, something she'd never heard from him in the whole sixteen years they'd been friends.

"What do you mean? You belong here, on the *Knox*. This is home."

He looked back at her, deep shadows in his gaze. The small smile he sent her looked bleaker than anything else.

"Emmanuel has my command. The *Valiant Knox* doesn't need more than one commander."

She bristled, crossing her arms as indignation swept through her. "Well then Commander Emmanuel can go back to whatever duty they pulled him from. You're back, this ship is yours. You worked your ass off every day for nine years to get that position."

He ran a hand over his short hair and dropped his gaze. "It's not that simple."

Would he be posted somewhere else? Would she lose him again when she'd only just gotten him back? Her stomach clenched over a churning sick feeling and without thinking, she reached out to take his hand.

"Don't worry about it now, Kai. Just get better first and then whatever happens, we'll deal with it."

He stared at her, his fingers tightening against hers. With a slow movement, he straightened up from the pillows and caught her chin. Her breath left her in a rush as he leaned toward her. Hadn't she just finished telling herself that kissing him could make things worse, not better?

"Kai—"

He closed his mouth over hers, cutting off the words. This time, there was no desperate plunge into lust. As if the other kiss had been a dream, the gentle, questioning movement of his mouth against hers seemed more real than anything she'd felt in the past eighteen months. For a second, the pressure and sensation of his lips against hers seemed totally foreign. But then a surge of warmth, of utter rapture erupted from her soul and spread through her body, filling her empty heart. She grabbed on to his shoulders and pulled herself closer, hard emotion coming on the heels of the initial exhilarated burst. In that moment, there were no words to describe how she felt about having him back. She could only repeat a litany of *thank you, God,* over and over in her mind.

Kai broke the kiss on an uneven breath. "God, Sacha, I missed you. I can't tell you how many days I sat in that cell and thought of nothing but you. And today…today you've brought me alive again."

Emotion clamped around her chest and surged upward to block her throat, making her eyes sting.

But now was the time to push her own needs and battered heart aside, to focus on the job of getting him better. Today was easy. The first day back, everyone was happy and riding the triumph of Commander Yang returning. Yet his simple question of *where do I belong?* foreshadowed just some of the difficulties he'd face in readjusting to life post-POW. She'd treated more than a few returned soldiers, and every one of them said things got harder as the weeks and months went by, not easier. Bringing any feelings into that equation would only make things messier.

His hand came up to touch the side of her face. "I'm sorry. I shouldn't have kissed you, or said those things. You're still mourning Elliot."

She lifted her head to meet his eyes, their faces only inches apart, determined to change the subject to something less emotional *for her*. More than anything, she needed to concentrate on Kai and his recovery, let him work through his losses, not hers. "What happened to Amos?"

Kai's gaze sliced away from her. "The morning I escaped, I woke up and he'd died sometime during the night. I have no idea what killed him. Take your pick, dehydration, starvation, the cold, the last beat-down he took from the guards. All of the above." He took a ragged breath, moisture gathering at the corners of his eyes where his thick lashes tangled together.

"You remember a few years back his arm got crushed, and you guys replaced most of the bones with alloy?" He closed his eyes and swallowed. "I cut a length of it from his forearm and used it as a weapon on the guards. That's how I escaped."

Horror stabbed right through her middle, followed by a wave of nausea. *God*. And that probably wasn't even the worst of what he'd been through while in the CSS prison. However, that incident alone could haunt a man the rest of his life.

She slid her hand across his chest and up his neck to cup his face. Tears trickled from his closed eyes and he clenched his jaw, before wiping them away with an angry swipe.

"Kai, you did what you had to in order to survive. Amos wouldn't hold that against you, *no one* would hold that against you. The fact that you used some initiative to escape instead of lying down in that cell and dying makes you a hero."

His eyes snapped open, fury lighting the depths, though it wasn't directed at her. "I got away on sheer luck. And now I get to live with the fact that I left a man behind. Not only that, but I mutilated the body before I went. So yeah, that sounds like hero material to me."

She clamped her lips together over the urge to argue. In this moment, he was hurting and wouldn't believe her no matter what she said. He might never see himself in that light. Except she knew once his story got out—and it would, the military loved a good survival story—he would become a renowned hero and the reputation of fearless Commander Yang would become the stuff of legends.

She let her hands drop. "I really should leave you to sleep."

He caught her wrists and stopped her from moving back. "I'll sleep, but only if you stay."

Her pulse thrummed through her and she arched an eyebrow at him. "So Commander Yang isn't above blackmail and guilt trips?"

He released one of her wrists to wrap an arm around her middle, pulling her off balance and more firmly against him. "That's right, and if Commander Yang says he wants his doctor in bed with him, then that's exactly what's going to happen."

The reminder of her position as a doctor was a cold slap in the face with reality. She pulled against his hold. "I'll just go get Macaulay then. Though I don't know how he's going to react to the news he has to climb into bed with you."

"You haven't changed a bit." Kai tightened his hold with a surprising amount of strength and kept her close. He caught her lips for a quick, hot and sweet kiss.

She wanted to reply that he hadn't changed either, but they both knew that wasn't true.

"All right, I'll stay to make sure you get some sleep. Let me just get all these machines hooked back up."

He let her go with obvious reluctance and she got busy hooking him back into everything to complete his healing process. By tomorrow, he'd be fully regenerated, though it would take some time to regain the muscle mass he'd lost. Still, all the nutrients and special healing white blood cells they were pumping him full of had filled him out a little and made his skin a healthy color. Made him look a bit more like his old self.

When she'd finished getting the BMC in place, she lowered the lights, kicked off her shoes, grabbed a spare blanket, and then hustled up next to him on the bed. He positioned his arm underneath her and half turned on his side, enveloping her in his warmth and strength.

She rested her head on the crook of his shoulder and snuggled deeper as her eyes dropped closed, the lids feeling heavy all of a sudden.

His breathing evened out almost immediately, and within a few minutes, the relaxed weight of his body told her he'd fallen asleep. Despite being comfortable enough to drift off herself, she carefully and quietly wiggled out of his hold, and then slid off the bed. She couldn't imagine anything better than staying snuggled up to him all night, but the best thing she could do for him was let the machines do their thing, and leave him in peace.

At the door, she stole a look over her shoulder, heart skipping a beat at the sight of him lying there. Ignoring her reluctance to leave, she gave orders for the nursing staff to leave Commander Yang be for a few hours—he needed uninterrupted sleep, not well-meaning check-ups every twenty minutes. With the job done, she left the room, not letting herself look back again.

With every step she took, she told herself that when she returned to the med-level tomorrow and walked into Kai's room, she would be Doctor Dalton, and that was all. No more kisses, and definitely no more showers together, or even the most innocent sponge bath. The nursing staff were supposed to handle that sort of thing. And if her chest tightened a little at the thought of someone else washing Kai? Well, she'd just add it to the long list of emotions to compartmentalize and ignore.

Chapter Five

Kai glared at the offending piece of rehab equipment, before directing the glower at the nurse holding it.

"Who ordered that?"

The nurse shuffled back a step. "Doctor Macaulay, sir. He said since you have refused surgery, you need this for at least the next week or you risk—"

"Tell Macaulay if he expects me to hobble around on a walking stick, he can damn well come and inform me himself. That way I can tell him in no uncertain terms where he can shove it."

The nurse nodded stiffly and then hurried out of the room, leaving the door open after she'd disappeared.

Kai dragged a hand over his face. Okay, the nursing staff didn't deserve a roasting over the fact they were trying to help him and acting under Macaulay's orders, but after the few unsatisfying hours of sleep he'd gotten last night, the day had dragged by, especially since Sacha hadn't put in an appearance.

One of the sub-doctors had mentioned something about back-to-back emergency trauma surgeries, but he'd been finding it hard to retain anything all day. Weird, but he'd think of something and then immediately forget it. Apparently it was something to do with his mind trying to process his sudden flight from captivity to returning to his old life, and should resolve itself shortly. In the meantime, it was damn frustrating.

Macaulay had told him not to leave his room, that he was supposed to be resting, but he'd spent the better part of the last eighteen months staring at the same four walls. The prospect of doing that again didn't appeal. Even if it was in a med-level room he could technically leave at any time he wanted.

The only problem? He had no shoes. And no shirt. Only the PJ bottoms he'd put on after his shower last night. A short search of the room didn't turn up anything else; the trolley Sacha had used to wash and shave him had been taken away at some point. Probably by Macaulay, the interfering douchebag.

Well, half the medical staff had already seen the scars of his captivity, physical and mental, considering his little meltdown over the drugs. It was stupid, logic told him that loud and clear. Anything the medico staff gave him would be safe, but even just the idea of taking medication made a cold sweat break out on his lower back. He shook his head at himself and made for the door. He needed to walk to distract himself and clear his mind. The more time he spent alone, the more he thought about *things* — things he couldn't change, things that wouldn't be good for him to dwell on.

Not to mention he'd just been through a marathon of sub-space calls with his parents and sister. Some of his extended family wanted to speak with him as well, but he just didn't have the emotional energy to deal with any more of that today.

Out in the passageway, he stepped into the path of a sub-doctor, who paused and cast what could have been an amused look over him.

"Somewhere you need to be, Commander?"

He cast around in his mind for the guy's name. "Moore, isn't it?"

The sub-doctor nodded with an irreverent grin. "Archibald, according to my personnel file. But I go by Archie, or Ace."

"Ace, of course. You're friends with the captain of the fighter force, right, Leigh Alphin? I think we've met before."

"Yes, sir, but it was a long time ago, and I seem to remember copious amounts of beer may have been involved."

Well, at least he could blame that memory lapse on being drunk, and not because the CSS Enlightening Camp had scrambled his brain.

"Could you tell me where I might find Doctor Dalton?"

Ace motioned over his shoulder. "Just coming out of surgery. End of the hall and turn right."

"Thanks." He held out his hand, and Ace shifted the datapad he was holding to his left to return the brief shake. "And if Doctor Macaulay asks—"

"I never saw you." Ace shot him one last grin before brushing by him and continuing down the hallway, disappearing into the room next to his.

Kai resumed his walk with more purpose, now that he

had a destination in mind.

When he reached the end of the corridor and turned right, like Ace had instructed, he came face to face with a door marked MEDICAL PERSONNEL ONLY. He reached up and pressed a palm to the door, intending to walk through, except those stenciled letters brought him up short. As the commander of the *Knox*, no part of the ship had been off limits for him. But he wasn't the commander anymore, and technically, as a patient of the hospital, he shouldn't go wandering into places he didn't have clearance. The full scope of that fact rounded out and compressed around his lungs. Likely no one would have the gall to tell him otherwise, if he went into those off-limit places, but his new status in limbo had him questioning his right to go anywhere he wanted.

Sacha had always teased him about going above and beyond to follow the rules, while Elliot had told him it was why he'd become one of the youngest commanders in the United Earth Force's history.

With reluctance, he lowered his hand, stepped back from the door, and turned away. It seemed his time as a POW hadn't changed some facets of his personality. He still couldn't break the rules.

Across from him was an alcove with some padded chairs and a small table. A vending machine took pride of place in the wall, offering beverages and snack foods. *Coffee*. His mouth literally watered at the thought of a strong, stinging, hot cup. The nurses wouldn't let him have any this morning, said he couldn't have anything except the multi-jelly until Macaulay told them otherwise. But this was one rule he had no hope in hell of following, not if it involved an honest-to-god cup of coffee.

He walked over and touched the screen. His fingers moved over the keypad almost automatically, and satisfaction rolled through him when it turned out that he'd not only remembered the crew code to access such things, but apparently they hadn't been changed since Emmanuel had taken over his post.

In another few moments, the machine had delivered his order, and he wrapped his hand around the cup, enjoying the slight burn of the hot drink against his palm as he picked it up.

"Is that for me? Thanks, I need it." Sacha reached around him and slipped the cup out of his hand.

He turned and sent her a glare as she blew at the steam, before taking a tentative sip. Her hair was a mess, and there were dark smudges under her eyes, but his heart thumped at the sight of her. He'd spent half the day telling himself he probably shouldn't have kissed her after only being back on the ship for a few hours. Yet he couldn't regret it, not when the simple pleasure of it had cleansed his soul in a way nothing else probably ever would.

No doubt it would cause complications; he'd seen others take the friends-to-lovers path, only to have things end in disaster. But Sacha was more than just his friend, she'd been a constant presence in his life for so long it felt like at some point she'd simply become a part of him.

He crossed his arms, unable to stir annoyance at her, even if she had stolen the first coffee he'd laid his hands on for almost a year and a half. "That was mine."

Although he tried for an affronted tone, the words came out sounding more amused than anything.

She took another sip and sent him a look that seemed to say *oh yeah?*

"Macaulay cleared you for something other than multi-jelly, did he? Well, I'll have to have a word to him about that, since technically you're my patient."

He crossed his arms. "Am I? Because I haven't seen you all day."

"I've been stuck in surgery since four a.m., but the staff has been giving me updates on you." Her gaze wandered down over his chest, all the way to his bare feet. "But I don't remember telling anyone you could walk around med-level half naked, ordering coffee."

He shifted his weight, awareness flashing through him at her casual perusal. When her gaze came back up to meet his, he sent her a frown, though it was only half serious.

"I was locked in the same small cell for over a year. Did you really think I was just going to sit around in my room when I'm feeling so much better?" He reached over and plucked the half-empty coffee from her hand. "And I can't remember the last time I drank coffee. You can go all Doctor Dalton on me, but if I don't get to drink what's left of this coffee, I'll probably tell you the same thing I told the nurse who tried to give me a walking stick."

She raised an eyebrow. "And what was that?"

"Just be glad you won't ever find out." He took a sip of the coffee and wanted to groan as the familiar bitter flavor hit his tongue and coated the back of his throat. There were some things he hadn't even realized he'd missed until he'd gotten back on the ship and been reminded of them.

"Commander Yang."

Kai turned to see Emmanuel headed toward him. The other commander stopped in front of him, and they exchanged a brief handshake. Grant Emmanuel was about ten years older than him, typical of most UEF commanders. His dark brown hair was speckled lightly with silver, and he had a shorter, stockier build. He'd met Emmanuel a handful of times before, at the bi-annual commanders' conference the UEF liked to hold.

"Good to see you up and around." Emmanuel stepped back and clasped his hands behind his back, sending a respectful nod toward Sacha. "I assume this means you're feeling well?"

"Compared to this time last week, I'm feeling great." He drained the last of the coffee and set the cup aside. "Was there something I can do for you, Commander?"

Emmanuel inclined his head, expression intent. "I know you only got back to us yesterday, but the UEF doesn't like loose ends."

"No, they certainly don't." The UEF liked their procedures, liked everything to run like clockwork in a neat, orderly fashion. It suited his personality perfectly, though he knew it often rubbed some people the wrong way. A commander coming back from the dead would be PR gold, but also the kind of mess they'd want dealt with quickly.

"I'll need you to come up to the command center tomorrow so we can discuss your situation." Emmanuel glanced at Sacha. "Make sure he's discharged by then, Doctor."

The gleam in Sacha's gaze suggested she'd discharge him when she was good and ready, but she nodded nonetheless. After all, she might have been med-staff, but she was still technically under Emmanuel's command. "Yes, sir. I'll see to it that he's sufficiently recovered by then."

"My thanks." Emmanuel inclined his head in her direction. "If you'll excuse me, I need to get back up. Yang, I'll be in contact with the time."

"Yes, sir." He saluted Emmanuel, even though they were of equal rank and he didn't have to under informal circumstances. Despite the underlying sting at the fact the man now had Kai's post, the hard years of military training wouldn't let him be anything but respectful.

Emmanuel returned the salute, before turning precisely on his heel and marching off down the corridor.

"Tell me I wasn't that uptight when I was in command?" he muttered as Emmanuel disappeared around a corner.

He glared down at Sacha, who was obviously trying not to smile. "I was *not* that stuffy."

She patted him on the shoulder, all condescending as hell. "No, you were worse."

"That is not even—"

Sacha laughed, and it was the best sound he'd ever heard, the echo of it rippling beneath his skin.

"I'm just joking, Kai. Maybe in another ten years the UEF will have shoved their very correct stick so far up your ass you'll be just like Emmanuel. But no, you weren't ever that uptight before."

"Thanks," he said, not sure if he should be insulted by her prediction for his future behavior. "What are you doing now? Want to share a meal?"

She shook her head, before pushing a strand of hair from the side of her face.

"Sorry, I've got post-surgery stuff I need to follow up on. I'll come and see you when I'm done, okay?"

Disappointment tightened his chest, but he kept his expression neutral. "All right, but make sure you eat something."

She rolled her eyes at him, just like she used to do when

they'd been teenagers.

"Fine, I'll eat. But you have to promise to eat every single multi-jelly the nurses bring you for dinner, and I'll be checking your file to make sure. I promise you can start on normal food tomorrow morning."

"Jelly again?" He sent her a disgusted look. The multi-jelly had been fine yesterday and even this morning for breakfast. But when they'd presented him with the same option for lunch, his growling stomach had yearned for something more substantial. After eating drugged slop at the CSS prison, it didn't seem right to bitch about living on jelly for a few days, but he could have killed for some meat and potatoes.

"Suck it up and take it for one more meal, Commander." Sacha shot him an impertinent grin. She pointed a finger at him. "And don't use the excuse that you're saving one for me just in case I forget to eat. Not even watermelon."

"You got me," he said, sending her an unimpressed look.

She wiggled her fingers at him before disappearing back through the door for medico personnel only.

He ran a hand over his short hair, still finding it a little odd he wasn't covered in months' worth of filthy shag. A couple of female sub-doctors and nurses stepped out of the door Sacha had disappeared through, stopping short when they saw him standing there.

He crossed his arms and stepped back, nodding a greeting as they passed. A couple of them shot him assessing stares over their shoulders, before whispering between themselves. Uncomfortable awareness welled within him. He hadn't felt self-conscious about walking around in only the PJ pants until that moment, and he couldn't remember the last time he'd been checked out, if that's what they'd been doing. There was every chance they were talking about his scars, or the fact that until yesterday they'd all thought he was dead.

So what happened when a dead man returned to life?

He was a commander who had nothing to command. He doubted the UEF had any protocol in place for that sort of thing. Surely it would take time for them to work out where he belonged now? But Emmanuel certainly hadn't wasted any time coming down here to tell him they needed to sort his *situation*, as if it were some kind of simple misunderstanding. Except this wasn't a military exercise gone wrong or strategic defense executed incorrectly, this was his life, his future they were talking about.

Had they already made a decision about him? Would he be leaving the *Knox* before he'd even gotten his footings back in reality? A coldness rippled under his skin. He shut down the thoughts, because his mind couldn't handle thinking about anything beyond another unsatisfying meal of multi-jelly. Yet the shadows of uncertainty had already formed in the back of his mind.

On a ship that had once been his, with hundreds of people going about their daily lives, he'd never once felt alone. Not like he did now.

• • •

Sacha pulled off her blood-splattered surgical gown with a tired sigh. She hadn't gotten through more than half an hour of her post-surgical follow up before the young soldier she'd been operating on had suffered complications, and she'd had to take him back in again.

It was almost midnight. Her back was aching and her eyes felt too dry, the way they always did when she got too tired and needed a solid few hours of uninterrupted sleep. She didn't want to do anything except change out of her scrubs into her own clothes, and escape to the peaceful sanctuary of her apartment and her bed.

Med-level was quiet and dim, the sparse number of night staff going through their duties with hushed efficiency. She had to pass Kai's room on the way out, and she paused outside his door. She'd promised she'd come see him when she was finished, but she couldn't have anticipated it would be so late. It wasn't likely he'd still be awake; his body needed the healing rest of sleep. Still, if he happened to ask her tomorrow, at least she could honestly say she'd looked in on him before she'd left for the night.

Sacha pressed the door release. A low light had been left on, so the room wasn't completely dark. She stepped forward, hesitating at the empty bed. Where the heck had he gone, off walking again? She could understand him not wanting to be cooped up in one room after he'd spent so long locked up without the most basic freedoms, but his recovery would be that much longer and harder if he didn't give himself time to heal.

Something caught her attention in her peripheral vision, halting her movement. Walking around the bed to get a clearer look, she saw Kai lying huddled in the corner where the floor met the wall.

His body was shuddering and she rushed forward, thinking he was having some kind of seizure. But as she came down on her knees next to him, she realized his body was quaking in the throes of a nightmare.

Her first instinct was to wake him up, but the doctor in her forced down that urge. She had no idea what he'd been through and no clue how shocking or frightening his dream might be—he could wake up violently. If she got hurt, even accidentally, he would blame himself and the guilt would be like adding acid to an already volatile cocktail.

The best thing she could do was ride it out with him. She pushed up and hurried over to the bed, grabbed a blanket, then returned to his side. She draped the blanket over him, and then settled cross-legged beside him, not out of reach, but far enough back that she could get out of the way if he moved suddenly.

She leaned forward a little and lightly set her hand on his shoulder. His T-shirt was damp, the edges of his hair darkened with sweat. He felt clammy and, beneath her palm, his muscles were so taut there could have been rock under his skin.

"It's all right, Kai," she whispered, her words short over the tightness in her throat. "I'm right here. I just need you to come back to me."

The tremors seemed to subside, his body losing some of the tension. Had her voice soothed him, or had it just been a coincidence and the nightmare had run its course? He groaned, the sound low and pained, echoing through her chest with a painful stab. She smoothed her hand over his shoulder and up his neck to cup the side of his face. The tautness in her throat swelled into a lump as she tugged up the corner of the blanket and used it to wipe away the tears leaking from beneath his closed eyelids.

"Whatever happened to you, I'll help you through it."

This time, her voice came out a strangled murmur, and she swallowed down the thickening urge to cry.

Kai had always been there for her, from the first day she'd met him as a petrified thirteen-year-old walking into a class of older students, sure she'd be a social outcast for the remainder of school. But he'd included her in his group of friends, making her high intelligence seem cool and interesting rather than the burden she'd always found it to be. If not for him, she would have spent her high school years in lonely misery, instead of ending up with the great friends she'd had.

Now he needed her to be the protective pillar in their friendship and she would do whatever it took to see him through this. She couldn't let her own emotions get the better of her, no matter what horrors he told her about the past year and a half he'd been away.

Kai's breathing altered slightly, and his eyelids flicked open. His gaze landed on her, shadowed with the confusion of sleep and his lingering nightmare.

"Sacha, what are you doing here?"

She took a quick breath to quell her own distress. "I came to check on you before I went home. You were having a nightmare."

He reached up and grabbed her elbow, his expression desolate. "You can't be here, it's not real."

She shifted onto her knees, bringing herself closer to him. "You're on the *Valiant Knox*, remember? You escaped."

He shook his head, his grip tightening on her. "No, it was just a dream, there's no way out. We tried over and over for months, but there is no escape, and there isn't any help coming. Then we realized…"

"What, Kai?" She set both hands on either side of his face, trying to get him to focus on her, but he seemed trapped in the nightmare that still had a grip on his mind. "What did you realize?"

"This is where we die."

Her chest contracted around her lungs, making her breath short, as she forced herself into his line of vision. "No, you escaped, remember? A patrol found you on the banks of the Wyre River. You said something about jumping off some rocks."

His attention shifted past her, his expression becoming confused. "Is this a med-room?"

Relief crashed through her, and she blew out a short breath. "Yes, you've been here two days."

He pulled out of her grasp, struggling to his feet.

"Where's Amos?" He cursed when he put his weight on his bad leg. She got in under his shoulder and wrapped an arm around his middle, helping him toward the bed. But he'd hardly sat down before he was getting back up again. "I have to see—"

She set both her hands against his shoulders. "Kai, Amos isn't here. He didn't leave the camp with you."

For a long moment he stared at her, and then she saw the memories return to him in the darkening of his gaze.

"Oh god, Sacha, what I did—" He pushed past her and rushed over to the sink, gagging several times, but not bringing anything up.

She gave him a moment, then walked over and reached past him to run a cup of water from the faucet. He braced his hands against the edge of the sink, his head hung low and breathing uneven. She set the cup down on the bench.

"What you did was survive, just like we talked about before." She kept her words low and quiet. "And, no doubt, we'll talk about it again."

"Because talking about it will make it all better, right?" The bitter cynicism in his voice came through loud and clear.

A small swell of frustration washed through her, but retreated just as quickly at the bleakness in his gaze.

"No, talking about it won't make what happened any better, but it will help you process things. Survivor's guilt is a slippery slope, and I don't want to see you get lost in it. You didn't kill Amos, you weren't responsible for what happened to him, and you couldn't have done anything differently. So please don't torture yourself playing the *what if* game."

Kai straightened, reaching for the glass and downing the contents in a couple of long swallows. He put the cup into the sink, avoiding her gaze, his posture tight and withdrawn.

"I can't imagine the things you're feeling, but blaming yourself won't help Amos, and it definitely won't help you." When she reached out to touch his shoulder, he shifted away from her.

"I'm well aware I can't change the past." His voice came out a little gravelly, and he still wouldn't look at her. He turned away from the sink and headed back across to his bed, giving off a definite *leave-me-alone* vibe.

She resisted the urge to keep pushing him, to walk over to the bed and offer him physical comfort. "I'm heading home for the night. If you need anything, buzz one of the nurses."

As he sat on the edge of the bed, he made a noise that could have been an agreement. Of course, he'd probably have to be almost dead before he did actually buzz for help, and even then he still might refuse to admit he needed it.

She'd always found his stubbornness kind of amusing, but then she'd never exactly come up against it like she had tonight.

She started backing toward the doorway. "I'll come by in the morning and make sure you get a real breakfast."

"Thanks, Sacha," he murmured, though considering his tone, he might as well have said *whatever, Sacha*.

She exhaled tiredly as she left his room and resumed the trek to her apartment. His despondency worried her, but pushing him wouldn't get her anywhere. His recovery was bound to be full of ups and downs, and she couldn't get herself into a panic every time he hit the slightest bump.

But the notion that he might try to push her away had lodged itself into her brain and refused to budge. He obviously hadn't wanted anything from her after coming out of that nightmare, a total reversal from last night, when he'd asked her to stay with him.

Had he been ashamed about her seeing him in such a state, or just determined that he'd deal with his demons on his own? Or perhaps he thought to shield her from the worst of what he'd been through. She'd seen it happen with other returned POWs. They felt guilty that they weren't the same person they'd been before and weighted under the pressure to be that person for their loved ones. Often it resulted in the person simply closing themselves off and ending up isolated.

Whatever the case, she wouldn't be so easily deterred, and Kai, of all people, should know that about her. It didn't matter that he wouldn't be the same man he'd been before he'd walked off the *Knox* and not returned.

The only thing that really mattered was that he was alive, and he'd come back.

Chapter Six

Sacha dropped down onto one of the fancy circular couches scattered about the large, airy anteroom outside the command center. She picked up a mediapad and absently scanned through the choices of newspapers and magazines on offer from the sub-space link-up. The news all looked depressing like usual, so she tabbed on a gossip mag, filled with celebrity stories that were probably all made up.

Officers and command staff came and went as she skimmed the contents of the rag. Every time the huge, gleaming, matte-silver double doors across the anteroom opened, she took a quick glimpse to see who was coming through. Only high-ranking military personnel got to go through those doors. Or someone with an escort of aforementioned high-ranking military staff. Most people didn't get to see the cushy high-end bar and restaurant that the top-notch service people of the *Knox* got to hang out in. Or the recreation facilities that lacked for nothing. A far cry from the measly cafeteria, gym, and TV room the doctors had.

As soon as Kai had been ranked high enough to get in to the sacred space, he'd often taken her and Elliot in to hang out with him. Most of the higher-ranking officers had been cool about it, and they'd all had some seriously fun times. She hadn't been through those doors since the day he'd disappeared.

The doors whooshed open again and this time when she looked up, she spotted Kai walking out toward her. His stride was still slightly uneven, and despite the fact he'd spent over twenty-four hours with the BMC on, the damage had been too great. In the end, she and Macaulay had both agreed unless he had surgery, he was going to have a small limp for the rest of his life.

She put the mediapad back on the chrome and glass table next to the couch and then stood as he reached her. In casual jeans and a plain navy colored T-shirt, he looked good, *great actually*.

The past few days of multi-jelly, plus a nutritional, and white blood cell treatment had brought him back to 100 percent health. She'd discharged him from the hospital a few hours ago and hadn't found the chance to talk with him since she'd walked into his room late last night and found him having that nightmare. When she'd stopped by earlier that morning to see how he liked the special breakfast she'd ordered up for him, he'd seemed determined to pretend like the night before hadn't happened.

"What are you up to?" Kai asked, bending to sit on the couch with a slight grimace. He rubbed a hand over the knee on his right leg.

"I just got off-shift and heard you'd gone to the meeting

with Commander Emmanuel and Captain Phillip. Thought I'd come up here and wait for you to come out. Is your leg still hurting?"

He grinned at her, though the expression had a pained edge to it. "Don't pull that doctor crap with me, Sacha. You just said you were off-shift."

She crouched down and grabbed his ankle. "Still, it shouldn't be hurting too much. I told you, we can go in and operate—"

He wrapped a hand around her upper arm and pulled her up. "And I said it's fine. I don't want surgery. It's just a dull ache. Nothing I can't live with."

"In this day and age, you shouldn't have to live with it." She crossed her arms and sent him an annoyed look as she sat down next to him.

"Change of subject."

She huffed a sigh. "Fine, how did your meeting with Emmanuel go?"

He avoided her gaze. "Uh-uh, not going there either. Pick a different topic. I know, how about dinner? You have plans?"

She laid a hand on his shoulder and waited until he looked at her. "Kai, come on. Tell me what happened. You are getting your post back, aren't you?"

He shoved a hand through his hair, jaw clenched in obvious tension. "They have no idea what to do with me. Hell, they don't even have anywhere to stick me now that I'm out of the med-level. They offered me a bunk in the cadets dorm, but I told them I'd rather pay my own way in one of the ship's hotels. That's assuming I even have any money I can access. Who knows what happened to my accounts and savings?"

Her heart clenched and she tightened her fingers on his shoulder. "Don't be an idiot. You're coming to stay with me."

He glanced at her sharply, several emotions crossing his face too fast for her to make sense of them before he blanked his features. "I don't want to put you out—"

"I said *don't be an idiot*. I'm your oldest friend. Who else is going to help you when you need it?"

"You've already done so much…"

"As your *doctor*. Don't make me slap some sense into you. Besides, I'm offering for my own convenience. This way I can monitor your recovery more easily."

A ghost of a grin lightened his features. "Only if you're sure."

She started to reply, but Kai's attention had shifted somewhere past her shoulder, as a perplexed look briefly crossed his face. Across the anteroom, Colonel Cameron McAllister was just stepping out of the transit-porter, along with a group of other highly ranked ground soldiers and military guards. The colonel oversaw the military post on the ground, but was technically still under the command of the *Valiant Knox*—for now that meant Commander Emmanuel, but of course, not that long ago, Kai had been his superior officer.

His expression closed off. Would this reminder of his old life drag down his already flagging spirit?

"Everything okay?" She tried to keep her tone conversational, with no concern whatsoever, but wasn't sure she'd made the mark as Kai snatched an unreadable look at her before standing.

"Yep. I just want to catch Cam before he goes into his meeting with Emmanuel." He stepped away from the couch she sat on and walked over to intercept the colonel.

McAllister looked happy to see him, and they did that manly back-slapping hug thing guys always did, before backing away from each other again. While they spent a few moments talking, she intently studied Kai's features to see if anything about the conversation was upsetting him. However, all she could read from his expression and manner was he seemed genuinely thrilled to be reconnecting with an old friend.

After a few moments, and some parting words about catching up, Kai moved back, allowing McAllister to continue on, his entourage following in his wake. Once they'd passed through the highly guarded doors into the command center, Kai returned to her side, a thoughtful look on his face, though it was definitely edged in uncertainty, as if he was trying to figure something out.

"Everything okay?" She swore at herself as the words popped out of her mouth again. If she kept this up, she was going to start sounding like a worried, nagging wife who couldn't leave well enough alone. And she'd never been one of those women, not even when Elliot had been alive.

"Yeah… It's just…when you see someone and you can't work out where you know them from?" He crossed his arms, gaze distracted inward as he obviously tried to jog his memory.

A spurt of worry erupted through her. Had his mind been affected more than they'd realized? Kai knew Cam almost as well as he knew her. "That was Colonel Cameron—"

He focused on her, an exasperated look crossing his face. "I'm not talking about Cam. I meant one of the military guard soldiers he had with him."

"Oh." She breathed a silent sigh of relief. Talk about immediate overreaction. She had to get a handle on jumping to the worst conclusions every time Kai seemed to present with something relating to his captivity. "Well, you probably just met him once, before you were captured."

"Probably, although I never dealt with many ground soldiers, apart from Cam and his higher-ranking officers." His brow creased, as if he was thinking even harder.

"If it was important, it'll come to you. Don't melt your brain trying to work it out in the meantime."

He stared down at her, one side of his lips lifting in a half grin. "Is that your medical opinion? I didn't realize brain melting was an actual risk of thinking too hard."

"Ha-ha, very funny." She pushed to her feet and leaned over to wrap her arm around his bicep. "Come on, you said something about dinner. If you're going to stay with me, take me out to *Assez Plaque* in return for lodging."

"That fancy French place? Did you just forget the earlier part of the conversation where I said I had no money?" He let her drag him over to the transit-porter, his reluctance obvious.

She rolled her eyes as she let his arm go to tap at the control panel for the transit. "Fine, dinner is on me. We'll go to Knox Steak and Grill instead."

He patted his stomach. "I could do with a juicy steak or two. *Real* steak, not the protein imitation stuff. And after that, I want to go to the movies and eat a huge tub of popcorn."

The transit-porter arrived and they entered, heading down to commerce level, an entire tier of the ship that doubled as a trading stop when the *Valiant Knox* wasn't stationed in a war zone, and offered everything from shopping to restaurants, bars and entertainment for the *Knox*'s staff who lived permanently on board.

"Looks like you've got the whole night planned." A flutter started in her stomach, as if she were a fifteen-year-old again. *Like a date.* Except not a date. Just two old friends catching up.

"While Emmanuel and Phillip try to work out what they're going to do with me, I might as well attempt to enjoy myself. If I tell myself it's a holiday, it won't seem so depressing."

Without thinking, she reached down and laced their fingers together. His words were casual, but she could hear the bleak tone underneath.

"Don't worry about it tonight. I think relaxing and enjoying yourself is a great idea."

He looked down at her with an intimate smile. She had to glance away and concentrate on the transit's display as a rush of warmth spread through her. She couldn't consider what tomorrow would bring, she just wanted to enjoy being with him.

• • •

Kai shoveled the last handful of popcorn in his mouth and set the empty container aside. On the cinema screen at the front of the room, the two main characters of the movie embraced in an emotional scene.

He looked down at Sacha, her head lolling against his shoulder, eyes closed, her breathing soft and even. He'd gone with her choice of a romantic comedy, not able to even stomach the thought of some hardcore action film, let alone sit through one. Except Sacha had fallen asleep not even fifteen minutes after the movie had started.

So he'd eaten the popcorn, slurped a sweet icy beverage all on his own, and gotten lost in the on-screen couple's comical problems standing between their relationship, instead of dwelling on where he knew that soldier from. Such a tiny detail shouldn't have mattered so much, but for some reason his mind had snagged on the man's face and left an unsettled sensation in the pit of his stomach. Like Sacha had said, if it was important, surely his brain would supply him with the information?

Maybe he'd seen or met the soldier the day he'd gone down to Ilari, where his patrol had been attacked and he and Amos had gotten captured. The soldier might have been part of the patrol, one of the injured soldiers they were able to save following the vicious fight. Kai swallowed down the chilling recollections and forced his focus to the story on screen.

When the credits rolled and people started getting up to leave as the lights brightened, he sat for a few seconds, enjoying the simplicity of the moment. Once the room had cleared, leaving him and Sacha alone, he shifted a little and ran a light touch over the side of her face.

"Time to wake up, Doctor Dalton."

Her breath hitched, her eyes rapidly blinking open as she straightened. She grimaced and wiped at some drool on the corner of her mouth. Kai clamped his jaw over the urge to grin at that. She'd always been a drooler when she slept.

"Did I miss the whole movie?" She glanced up at the screen and then around at the empty rows of seats.

"Looks like."

She frowned at him. "Why didn't you wake me up? I could have slept at home and not wasted twenty-five credits on a ticket."

He shrugged and pushed to his feet, forcing himself not to wince over the dull ache in his bad leg. She would just harass him about getting surgery again. Maybe one day he'd consider it. Right now, he couldn't stomach the thought of getting knocked out for the procedure, not after enduring the CS Soldier's game of randomly-spike-the-food.

"I was the one who wanted to stuff myself with popcorn and forget about everything for a while. Besides, you looked like you needed it after spending all day in surgery yesterday and going home so late last night."

Crap, that was the closest he'd come to mentioning their little midnight interlude, when she'd found him curled up on the floor and whimpering like a baby, not to mention the whole nearly-puking thing when he'd remembered what he'd done to Amos. He'd been cold to her afterward. Part of him had worried he might hurt her feelings, but it was the only way he could have gotten her to leave before giving into the burning urge to beg her to climb in bed and stay with him again.

And he refused to succumb, not after he'd woken up alone the morning before to find she'd left him sometime during that first night. It signaled her intentions loud and clear—she might be willing to look after him, to be the friend she'd always been, but anything else would be pushing it. Understandable, considering she'd buried her husband less than a year ago.

Still, as her annoyed expression melted away to regard him with something too close to tenderness, the smoldering urge to kiss her intensified. What was he doing? Even if she'd happened to indicate she felt the same way about him, the last thing he wanted was to give her ideas about anything between them.

He didn't know where the hell he fit in life anymore, so it wasn't like he was in a place to be starting anything. *If* he wanted to start something.

All the separate factors of his life were about to collide and make one hell of a mess. He needed to get that cleaned up before he worked out where he stood with Sacha. Except, that logic didn't stop the low burn of pure, carnal lust spreading through his veins and punching him hard in the guts every time he looked at her.

For about the hundredth time, he told himself staying at her place would be a bad idea. But the only other option was that damn bunk in the cadets dorm. He didn't need to lie awake at night while the infants tiptoed around him because they'd heard of *badass Commander Yang* and were terrified of putting a foot wrong.

She stood and stretched before rubbing her lower back with a cringe. "*Ow.* Cinema seats don't make for good sleeping."

She shuffled past him and he fell into step behind her when she led the way out of the empty room to the lobby where other movie-goers were milling. Sacha cut her way through the crowd ahead of him, saying hello to people here and there. Most people cast him wary or amazed looks, then spoke in hushed tones to one another. No prizes for guessing the topic of their discussion. He sighed with quiet despondence. *Better get used to that, soldier.* He'd become the topic of the decade: The Commander Who Returned from the Dead.

Sacha seemed too sleepy, so he didn't try to make small

talk with her as they went down into the residential levels of the ship. As they approached her door, which slid open at the remote sensor, too many memories crowded his mind. They all smashed together and congealed into one giant ball of stuff he didn't want to think about. He'd only been gone a year and a half, yet so much had changed. Despite longing for the simplicity of how things used to be, they could only move forward from here. However, reminding himself of that didn't lessen the moment of awkwardness at crossing the threshold into what had once been Elliot and Sacha's home.

He paused just inside the door as Sacha sighed, the sound relieved, and shrugged out of her light coat. She emptied her pockets onto a hall table and then kicked off her shoes. He caught sight of her toes wiggling against the carpet before she crossed to the sofa. For some stupid reason, the sight of her bare feet rammed home the intimacy of being alone in her apartment.

Her ottoman doubled as a storage chest and she bent to lift the lid and pull some blankets out. "You've slept on our couch before. Or should I say, passed out drunk. Either way, it'll probably be as uncomfortable as you remember. Sorry, Elliot and I never got around to applying for a bigger apartment with a spare room or two."

He walked forward and took the pile of blankets she held out to him. "Why would you need a bigger apartment?"

A strange expression crossed her face, part guilt, part ruefulness, a good dose of regret.

"Elliot and I were trying to get pregnant. We were going to start a family." A sad smile appeared for a brief moment. "He wanted to have a boy, and name it after you."

All the air left his lungs, like everything breathable had

been sucked out of the atmosphere. If Sacha had punched him, it would have felt exactly the same way. The raw shock must have shown in his expression, because she backed up a large step, ripping her gaze from his.

"I'm sorry, I shouldn't have told you that. Obviously I need to shut my mouth and go to bed. I'm on early shift, so I'll try not to wake you if you're still sleeping when I get up."

He couldn't find any words, instead just watched as she hurried across the small sitting area and shut herself in her room.

Kai's arms gave up and he dropped the blankets on top of the ottoman. Then his knees went the same way and he sat heavily on the edge of the couch.

Jesus…goddamn.

Sacha and Elliot had planned to have kids…and they'd talked about naming one after him. It hadn't happened obviously, but knowing that just made him feel a whole lot worse. He didn't want to feel guilty about kissing her, about *wanting* her. It didn't feel wrong, it felt *so right*.

He hated that Elliot had been killed. But in direct, aching contrast to that, he'd never been more relieved for anything in his life.

Which makes you a damned bastard.

He shoved the thought down and away, locking it up with all the other things he couldn't face yet.

The idea of being with her soothed the fractured pieces of his soul. Made him feel like it didn't matter if he was broken, if he wasn't the same man any longer…if he didn't get his goddamn command back from Emmanuel.

A quiet, cynical laugh escaped him. He didn't even know if he *wanted* his command back. What would he even do with it? The thought of engaging in any type of battle, of having to go down to the ground and oversee things on Ilari, of having to make decisions that would affect other soldiers' lives, made a roll of nausea swell through him like he'd just eaten a plate of gray slop from the CSS prison.

He clenched his jaw over the urge to gag. Somehow, he had to find a way around these feelings hampering him, because if he didn't have command of the *Valiant Knox*, if he wasn't a soldier, then who the hell was he?

The only other option was to put himself to pasture, take a brass position like the other commanders too old to actively serve any longer and spend his days spinning positive media for the UEF, attending fundraising functions and other shallow endeavors—pretty much becoming the UEF's arm candy.

But could he really live with putting himself into such a trivial position when he hadn't even turned thirty-five yet? That question overloaded his brain, making pressure pound behind his eyes.

Stop goddamn thinking. He forced his mind blank and bent to unfasten his boots before dragging one of the blankets from the pile. He punched a cushion into place and then lay down. After a few minutes, the light sensor beeped when it detected no movement and plunged the room into muted darkness.

His mind whirled, but he tried to keep himself distanced from the problems plaguing him. He couldn't do anything about them right now. The only thing he could do was try and get some decent sleep so he had a clear head to deal with things tomorrow. He stared up at the darkened ceiling.

It was going to be a long night.

Chapter Seven

Sacha flung herself onto her back and glared over at the clock display next to her bed. Three hours since she'd escaped Kai and she didn't feel the littlest bit sleepy.

Why the heck had she told him about her and Elliot's baby plans?

Things were alternately awkward and old-times-comfortable between them. They were on precarious ground, which threatened to crumble at any second. With what she'd blurted out, she got the feeling she might have just kicked the one stable rock from underneath them.

With a silent curse, she sat up and put her face in her hands.

"Stupid, stupid, stupid," she muttered into her palms.

At the sounds of movement and glass clinking from the sitting room, she stopped her litany and looked up at the door.

For the past few hours, she'd been wondering how she

was going to make herself face Kai in the morning. Yet the urge to talk with him right that second, maybe clear the air a bit, struck her so hard and fast she'd gotten out of bed and crossed the room before she'd quite thought about it.

As the door opened, she caught him midway between the couch and the kitchen. He froze when he saw her, a glass in one hand and a bottle of bourbon in the other. His hair stuck out all over the place, his gaze a little bleary, and he wore nothing but a pair of boxer briefs.

Her mind stumbled over that detail, so she forced her gaze to remain steady on his face.

"I'm sorry about before. I shouldn't have told you those things. It doesn't help or change anything. Although, drowning your sorrows probably won't help much either."

He dropped his attention to the bottle in his hand and then moved to set the glass down on a side table. "You should be able to talk about Elliot. He was your husband. I should be the one apologizing for reacting badly. You just surprised me, that's all. I guess I knew you'd probably have kids eventually. I suppose the whole naming-the-baby-after-me thing was the clincher."

Sadness pinched at her, but damned if she could get a clear idea on what had her so upset. The baby she'd never conceived? The fact that maybe Kai didn't like the idea of having a kid named after him? The confusion over her standing here wanting the man she'd always unknowingly cared for? The numerous reasons why letting herself get involved with him would be purely selfish?

She'd never realized how she'd relied on him simply being there until he hadn't been anymore. Hadn't known how deep her feelings for him really ran until she thought he'd been killed. Because part of her heart had definitely belonged to another man.

Then Elliot had been killed and the guilt had heaped on even worse. Because she'd mourned both men equally. Shouldn't she have felt more loss over her husband? Shouldn't the fact that Elliot had been taken from her shredded her soul? But it'd been Kai disappearing first that had done the real damage. By the time she got the news about Elliot, she'd gone into a kind of numb haze. The first few months after that were a blur in her memory.

And now Kai had returned, whole and alive. Deep inside, new life had started unfurling within her. Yet at the same time, the clash of elation and remorse made her head ache, pressure building up to combusting point within her.

You should feel awful. Because she wanted to grab on to him and hold on for all she was worth. Yet in this situation, she had to be the strong one, had to hold him up until he'd found his feet again. And the only way to do that was not let herself feel too deeply. Yes, Kai was her oldest friend, and there were emotions and sentiments attached to that she'd never be able to deny. But she had to keep her head above water, because sinking into her emotions wasn't the way to help him heal.

She dropped her gaze away from Kai, since looking at his almost-naked body made her heart pound too hard. "Sorry, I shouldn't have brought it up. How about when we see each other in the morning, we pretend like none of this ever happened?"

Before he could answer, she spun back toward her room, making a hasty escape so she could be alone with the aching guilt. But she barely made it through the doorway when two large, warm hands closed around her upper arms. The sensation of his fingers tightening into her bare flesh sent a swell of knee-weakening desire through her.

"Sacha, don't run away from me. I'm the one who should apologize. This is your home, and I've upset you."

"It's fine. Really, I've got an early shift in the morning," she mumbled toward the floor. She tugged against his hold, but he held her gentle and tight, not giving an inch.

God, she didn't want to deal with him right now, not when she felt so exposed, so worn down, and so damn confused. All of a sudden, keeping up the remorse over the emotions that had bombarded her in the past few days since Kai had dropped back into her life was exhausting. She just wanted things to be *simple*.

She sagged, giving up on the idea of fleeing Kai unless she wanted to get into an all-out struggle to break free. As she relaxed, he moved into her, bringing his chest up against her back. His hands loosened and then smoothed down her arms and back up again in a tender yet charged stroke.

Damn her to hell, but it felt so good to have the raw, masculine warmth of him against her. She turned into his embrace with a long sigh as her eyes slid closed.

Kai's hand came up to touch the side of her face. "I'm sorry, I'm being a selfish bastard. You're still mourning Elliot."

She shook her head and swallowed over the lump in her throat. "I *should* be mourning Elliot, and I feel so guilty that I'm not thinking about him as much now that you're here. I mean, you're alive! Part of me wonders when I'm going to wake up."

His topaz eyes darkened to a deep gold. "Did you dream of me when I was gone? I dreamed of you. Those visions kept me sane."

She nodded, her eyes watering. "When they declared you KIA, it broke my heart, Kai."

His hand slid partway into her hair, tightening subtly. She took a hiccupping breath, but stubbornly kept a lid on her emotions; partly because she got the feeling if she gave in to the urge to cry, she might not be able to stop.

"I'm a horrible wife, because when I lost you, it made me realize exactly where you always were. In my heart."

He clenched his jaw, looking as torn over things as she felt. But he didn't say anything. Instead he pulled her tighter against his chest. She rested her forehead on his pecs and let a few tears leak free.

"Elliot wouldn't want you to spend the rest of your life beating yourself up over this. You didn't betray him on purpose. In fact, you never betrayed him at all."

She felt the low words rumble through his chest. With his arms wrapped around her, contentment blossomed and spread within her.

"That's easy for you to say," she grumbled. However, his statement made her feel better about things.

"I spent the past year and a half hanging on to the memory of my best friend's wife like a lifeline. Don't you think I wondered how in the hell I could ever face Elliot again if I got out? How I would face *you*? I'd dream about you and then spend days wallowing in guilt. Amos thought I was a total ass." His warm breath ruffled her hair, sending a shiver rippling through her. "I hate to see you so upset, especially when I've been the cause."

"None of this is your fault, Kai. How could it be? All you did was make it back alive when everyone thought you were dead. We should be celebrating."

Tension leeched out of her muscles as his strong fingers lightly massaged her upper arms and shoulders.

"Then why do I feel like I should count my sins and wonder how I'll ever atone for them?" The catch in his voice made her heart clench, and she raised her head to look up at him.

"You're not the bad guy here."

His jaw clenched under a stubborn look. "Oh yeah? Then neither are you. I won't let you be."

She opened her mouth to argue, but his lips caught hers in a hard kiss, cutting off the words before she could so much as make a noise.

Reckless desperation exploded. Sacha gripped the back of Kai's neck. She refused to think anymore, she just wanted to *feel*. Because this, right here, was simple. She'd been alone in misery and numbness for so long, just going through each day without any real direction.

And then Kai had come home.

His arms dropped to close around her waist and drag her harder against him, thighs, hips and chests pressed so firm together she couldn't draw a full breath. But she didn't want to breathe. She wanted to consume every heated, exhilarating, wild sensation igniting between them, let it warm her cold heart.

He half picked her up and turned just far enough to get them to the couch. He kept her steady as he lowered her to the cushions and then came down on top of her, his mouth never breaking from hers for even an instant.

She let her hands loosen from their grasp on him and ran them over the lean contours of his muscled chest. The long-forgotten sensation of warm male skin under her fingers sent a shudder through her, made her insides clench with yearning and a bittersweet awareness of exactly what she'd been missing.

Her heart sped into orbit when he at last moved his mouth from hers, and laved hot kisses just under her ear and down her neck as he tugged at the tank top she wore for pajamas. A sense of familiarity clashed with the thrill of something new. This was *Kai*. Her oldest friend, so familiar in his scent and mannerisms, even the hitch of his breath felt achingly recognizable. But she'd never had this with him, never let what had been a tiny spark between them rouse into an uncontrolled inferno. Into the most beautiful, thrilling thing she'd ever imagined.

He tugged her top free and flung it aside, wasting no time in closing his mouth over her hardened nipple. She cried out in part surprise, part elation. Spasms of pleasure forked out from the pressure of his mouth, down into her lower abdomen.

Sacha pressed herself harder against him as she threaded fingers into his hair, while his hand caught the waistband of her pajama shorts. She shuddered at the light press of his knuckles against the skin at her hip, anticipation swelling toward the moment he'd pull the last of her clothes off, leaving her shamelessly naked and reveling in the friction of his skin against hers.

Sucking in a sharp breath, he stilled above her. It took her hazy mind a moment to realize he seemed frozen in place.

"Kai?" She cupped her hand along his jaw and urged his head up so she could see his face. His eyes were closed, expression a tight grimace. "What's wrong?"

He forced out a short, humorless laugh, and pushed up from her. "My damned leg."

"What's your pain level?" She scrambled upright as he shifted with stiff movements to stretch his injured leg out and set it on the ottoman.

"Damn it to hell, I'm not scaling my pain for you, Sacha." He avoided her gaze as he rubbed at his knee and upper calf.

Heart thrumming, she got up to retrieve her tank top and then went to the kitchen to find an ice pack. Heat flushed up her neck, because *oh god*, had she really just jumped him like a horny teenager? Forgotten everything she'd vowed about distancing herself for the sake of his recovery? She took a moment to press the ice pack against her heated face before returning to the couch.

His expression had eased somewhat, and there didn't seem to be as much tension in the line of his shoulders.

"Where does it hurt the worst?"

Kai looked up at her, and then glanced at her hand. "I'll take that."

She swallowed over a tightening throat as he held a hand out for the ice pack. A second ago they'd been all over each other, and now he didn't even want her to touch him? Yep, tossing logic into space and losing her head to heedless lust had been a *great* idea.

She reluctantly handed over the ice pack. "I can do that for—"

He lobbed the pack over his shoulder and then speared her with a stubborn glare. "My leg is fine. I don't need you to be my doctor. I need you to come back over here. And take all of your clothes off while you're at it."

She took half a step back, every muscle in her body tightening as she fought the urge to do exactly what he'd so unceremoniously ordered.

"No, I'm sorry that happened, but it shouldn't have. You *do* need me to be your doctor, and I shouldn't have forgotten that. And, for what it's worth, your doctor is ordering you to put that ice pack on your leg and get some rest. Without the benefit of that bourbon."

Before he could reply, she turned away from him, snatched up the bourbon, and headed for her room, trying for a sedate pace so it didn't look like she was running. Which she totally was.

"Sacha."

Her name in that low, exasperated tone of his shivered all the way down her spine, but she refused to look back as she made it to her bedroom door.

"Sacha, wait."

She stepped inside and passed her hand over the door control, thumbing the lock icon for good measure. A pounding on the panel a second later made her jump.

"Sacha, I'm sorry. Would you just come back out here so we can talk?"

Talk? Hah. Whatever kind of *talk* he had on his mind, she doubted it would feature many words. She took a considering look at the bottle of bourbon in her hand, before giving a small shrug and then knocking back a mouthful. After that short, but explosive, scene on the couch with Kai, she could use something to take off the edge.

He tried banging for another few moments, but when she didn't reply, he muttered a curse and gave up.

With a few choice words of her own, Sacha abandoned

the idea of bed, and curled up in the armchair in the corner of the bedroom, nursing the bottle of bourbon. Yeah, that wouldn't bode well for her early shift tomorrow, but right now, getting through the night without giving in to the urge to throw herself into Kai's arms seemed more important.

. . .

Sacha shifted, her body stiff, a crick in her neck shooting pins and needles into her shoulder. She blinked open her eyes and lifted her heavy head, recognizing her bedroom, but not understanding the current view she had.

She groaned and rubbed her nape, the movement causing something to slosh in her lap. She swore, glancing down at the bottle of bourbon, some of which was dripping down her thigh. With another low curse, she set the bottle on the floor and used the hem of her tank top to wipe the spillage off her leg. She hadn't drunk that much after escaping Kai and the moment they'd shared on her couch, but combined with her exhaustion, it had been enough to put her lights out for the rest of the night.

Her thoughts felt sluggish, her mouth bitter with the aftertaste of the alcohol. She pushed herself up, grimacing when the sudden movement made her brain spin. Oh god, she needed a few more hours sleep, but a glimpse of the clock told her she was due on-shift at med-level in half an hour. Just enough time to grab a shower and hopefully sneak out while Kai was still sleeping.

They needed to talk about what had happened, to make sure they both understood neither of them were in a position to consider intimacies between them, but she couldn't do it this morning when her mind felt woolly and her body frustratingly on edge with thwarted desire. She considered a cold shower, but that would only make her crankier.

Once she made it to the bathroom, she gulped down a glass of water and then forced her mind to go over some of the things she had to catch up on today. In no time at all she was dressed and sneaking out of her bedroom.

Except the sneaking part had been a waste of time. Kai sat fully dressed on her couch, watching some kind of morning news program and shoveling cereal into his mouth. His messy hair suggested he hadn't showered—still, he looked too good perched on the edge of the cushions, leaning over the coffee table where he also had a plate of toast and steaming mug sitting. The idea of climbing into his lap to finish what they'd started last night flashed hot and fast through her mind.

Her lungs stalled, and she forced her mind back into work mode, trying to resist the heat rising up through her chest and neck.

"Good morning." There, that had come out totally normal sounding.

He shot her a brief look before returning his attention to the screen.

"Morning, there's coffee brewed if you want to grab some before you go." His tone of voice was almost indifferent, totally at ease, as if they did this every morning and hadn't almost gotten naked and horizontal together just a few hours before.

"Thanks." How could he be so at ease sitting there, when she was all but floundering in her damned desires, which refused to be ignored? But she had to force them down, had to find an apathetic, but professional way of dealing with him while he was staying in her apartment, despite the inferno that had exploded between them last night.

She walked through the sitting room and found her work mug and travel lid already sitting on the counter next to the coffee pot. The sight stumped her, making her freeze in place. Elliot had never once done that for her in all the years they'd been together. It wasn't because he didn't care, she knew he'd loved her and he'd done plenty of other thoughtful things for her. But the smaller stuff had often escaped his notice.

Sacha took a short breath, telling herself it didn't mean anything, and then stepped forward to fill the mug with coffee. Just as she was finishing, her med-comm beeped and vibrated.

She quickly set the coffeepot down and pulled it off her belt, just as Kai stepped into the kitchen and placed his empty bowl in the sink.

"Getting calls already?"

She scanned the screen. "It's a bravo-orange code. They need me on the flight deck, port level alpha."

"One of the fighter pilots has been injured?"

"That would be my guess." She quickly snapped the lid onto her mug. "I have to go."

She brushed past him, hurrying to the hall table where she always left her things for an easy grab on the way out.

"I'm coming."

She glanced back at Kai as she shrugged into her coat. He was yanking his boots on, one hand braced against the arm of her couch for balance.

"You can't. I don't know what I'll find up there—"

He stalked over and stopped in front of her, his expression determined and as close to his old Commander Yang persona as she'd seen him.

"I might not have a current posting, but I retain my rank and, not so long ago, this was my ship and my people. I'm coming. I won't get in your way, but if there's anything I can do to help, I'm not going to sit here in your apartment watching morning trash TV."

She swallowed a sigh as she picked up her coffee again. She could refuse Kai as long and loudly as she liked, but he'd still do whatever the hell he wanted, especially when he got that look on his face. His unfailing tenacity had been one of the reasons he'd succeeded in becoming one of the UEF's youngest commanders in history, and the same fortitude of will was probably why he'd survived the CSS Enlightening Camp and made it back to the *Knox*.

"Fine, but once we're on deck I'm in charge, so you better be prepared to take my orders."

He sent her a grin and a quick salute. "Yes, ma'am."

Usually, she would have shot a comeback at him for that *ma'am* quip; instead she settled for sending him an exasperated glare, before hurrying out of her apartment.

Neither of them spoke as they made their way up into one of the top tiers of the ship that housed several levels of flight decks, plus amenities for the fighter pilot squadron and other flight-force contingents.

As they came out on port level alpha, where the majority of the fighter jets were hangared, a stream of people passed them—non-essential personnel being directed off deck as per emergency protocols. Good. If the crew were already following procedure, it made her job that much easier.

"There's Alpha." Kai pointed past her shoulder to where Captain Leigh Alphin, the CAFF—Captain of the Fighter Force—seemed to be in charge of organizing the deck into some kind of systematic chaos. She wasn't sure when he'd earned the nickname Alpha. He'd had the moniker for as long as she'd known him.

She brushed by the few flight-deck personnel still milling around and hurried over to his side. Sub-Doctor Moore had beaten her there and was already in conversation with the CAFF.

"What's the sit-rep?" she asked, coming to a stop beside them.

Alpha turned to her as he wiped at the sweat dampening his hairline. He was still in his flight jacket, though it was partway open, and beneath, his uniform shirt appeared damp. Must have been one hell of a firefight if Alpha had been on edge.

"We were on our way back from dead-watch patrol when a squadron of CSS vessels engaged us. We got all our fighter jets back on deck, but three came in on auto-retrieval. The last is just docking now; we don't know what the status of the pilots is. The deck maintenance crew are making sure the other two V-29s are safe to approach."

She focused her attention on Sub-Doctor Moore. "Let's assess before we move. We'll need easy access to those hatches as soon as the deck crew have cleared the jets."

"I'll get a couple of maintenance platform lifts." Alpha signaled a nearby soldier, and then noticed Kai standing nearby, who'd stayed so silent she'd almost forgotten he'd followed her up here.

"Commander Yang!" Alpha brushed by her to grab

Kai's hand, yanking him in for a quick embrace. "Sorry I haven't come to see you before now. It's good to have you back."

Kai replied, but Sacha didn't hear it as the maintenance chief called out that the two V-29 jets already docked were clear. She rushed toward the nearest one as a couple of deck hands maneuvered a platform lift next to the ship.

Chapter Eight

Kai watched as Sacha snapped into doctor mode, climbing onto the platform lift and getting up next to the cockpit of the V-29 fighter jet as someone popped the hatch off the top.

He glanced back at Alpha, who was watching the proceedings with a grim frown.

"Did you say the CSS engaged you?"

Alpha's expression tightened. "Close enough to the edge of the safe zone that they might as well have been inside it."

As he processed this information, Kai rubbed a hand over the lower half of his face, and the whiskers he hadn't found time to shave off in the last two days abraded his fingers. Things had changed dramatically in the year and a half he'd been gone.

Ever since the *Valiant Knox* had arrived at Ilari several years ago, they'd been systematically targeting the support bases of the CSS's organization; things like communications, supply drops, and ammo stations. The CSS had held their lines, but never actively engaged or launched any kind of offensive.

"Since when did they go on the attack?"

Alpha shrugged one shoulder. "A few months ago, they started with random air attacks on both armed and unarmed UEF ships. McAllister reported they'd also started offensives on the ground. We get the feeling they're working their way up to something big. So far none of our Command Intelligence agents have come up with anything."

An unsettled feeling streamed through him at this news and he crossed his arms, returning his attention to where Sub-Doctor Moore had joined Sacha on the platform next to the jet, working to get the injured pilot out of the damaged aircraft.

Lieutenant Teresa Brenner, Alpha's XO, approached, saluting both of them.

"Report?" Alpha asked shortly.

"Ace reported that Corporal Hays is deceased. He and Doctor Dalton are working on Orman, and the deck chief is clearing Dryden's jet now."

Alpha swore under his breath, dragging a hand across the lower half of his face. "Stay on it, Bren."

She returned the nod before turning and heading over to the platform lift, where Sacha and Moore had gotten Orman out of the cockpit and onto a stretcher.

"Sorry, Leigh." Kai clamped a hand on Alpha's shoulder for a moment. Losing any man was hard, but when it was one under direct command, he knew too well the deep gouge every single one could leave on a man's soul.

"Those CSS bastards are going to pay." Alpha shot him a sideways glance burning with ferocity. "Though I don't need to tell you that."

Yeah, the idea of revenge had kept him running hot after he'd first been captured, but now it left him feeling hollow. He didn't want to get some simple payback on those directly responsible for his imprisonment or the death of the fighter pilot here today. He wanted to systematically take apart the CSS from the top down and free the planets barely surviving in poverty under the control of the tyrannical regime. That had been the original goal of the UEF when this war started two decades ago, though no one could have guessed the conflict would end up encompassing so many worlds, or that the hostilities would go on for so many years.

Kai said, "Come on. Let's get some food into you. There's nothing you can do here until Sacha's seen to your men."

Alpha nodded tightly before the two of them turned and left the launch bay.

Neither of them spoke again until they got to the upper messdeck the pilots and other flight staff used. They'd arrived at the end of the rush of people getting breakfast before heading off to forenoon watch.

Even though he'd eaten already, Kai helped himself to a coffee and a pastry, while Alpha loaded up a plate. They sat down at a nearby empty table and Alpha used his fork to rearrange some of the food in front of him.

"I'm sorry you had to come back to the news about Elliot." Alpha looked up at him with a grim expression. "He was a reckless son of a bitch at the best of times."

He sent Alpha the ghost of a smile, even though mention of Elliot made guilt tighten in his chest at his current living arrangements with Elliot's wife...not to mention the fact he'd almost had sex with her on what had once been Elliot's couch. Yeah, that was something he didn't want to consider too closely. He should be mourning his friend, not trying to get into his wife's bed.

"Sacha told me how it went down."

Alpha shook his head and looked back down at his untouched breakfast. "I tried to check in with her as often as I could once Elliot was gone, especially since you were missing as well, but that woman doesn't make it easy. She kept insisting she was fine, even though anyone could see she wasn't. You know, she tried to convince me that *I* was the one who needed grief counseling."

Kai gave a short laugh at Alpha's rueful look. Yeah, that was Sacha, always trying to look after everyone else and putting herself last.

"Thanks, buddy. I'm glad you were looking out for her, even if she didn't want you to."

Alpha nodded, then dug into his post-dead-watch meal. Neither of them attempted any more conversation, but this was exactly what he'd missed all those months—the easy companionship of sharing a few quiet minutes with a friend and not needing it to be anything more than that. Sacha might try to tell him he needed to talk things out in order to heal, and partly that was true. But hanging out with his old friends and colleagues while *not* talking about anything much would help get him back on stable ground as well.

Alpha was just scraping his plate clean when Bren approached, holding a coffee in one hand and a datapad in the other.

"Dryden was conscious and in pretty good shape when they got him out of the jet. Mostly it was his controls that had been shot, which was why he came in on auto-retrieval.

Both he and Orman have been taken down to med-level, and Emmanuel's waiting in your wardroom for a briefing."

As he stood, Alpha shot Kai a grateful look. "Thanks for breakfast, want to catch up for a beer or two later?"

"Sure thing. Until someone works out what to do with me, I'm a free agent."

Amusement crossed Alpha's face. "Don't let it go to your head."

Kai sent the CAFF a short wave, watching as he and Bren left the messdeck, which was almost empty.

Now what did he do with himself? This was the first full day he'd been left to his own devices. Sacha would be on-shift for at least the next six hours, and anyone else he might want to catch up with would similarly be on duty, or sleeping if they were on night roster.

He looked down at himself, the T-shirt he'd been wearing since he was discharged yesterday looking a little on the wrinkled side. A nurse had scrounged up these clothes, so who knew where they'd come from. He needed to get some basics, before Sacha did something helpful like offer him Elliot's clothes. That was a line he would not be crossing. Something fresh was definitely on the cards.

Unfortunately, without any money, he couldn't buy anything on commerce level. A quick comm-call informed him that he needed to go into a branch in person with some ID to start getting the problem sorted out. At least they hadn't told him straight out that they couldn't help him.

On commerce level, he had to stop and check an info screen to find the bank, because he'd never actually been into the ship's Bank of United Earth branch since he'd taken his post on the *Knox* nine years ago; he'd usually done all of that stuff online. Once he knew where he was going, he set off, weaving through the sparse crowd. With only the *Knox*'s staff to service while they were stationed at Ilari, commerce level wasn't ever very busy.

Halfway there, a soldier wearing the ground forces uniform caught his attention—the same guy from yesterday he'd been trying to identify. Once again, a strange unsettled sensation swept through him, leaving a chill in its wake. Where did he know that soldier from? The harder he thought about it, the more it bugged him because his subconscious refused to cooperate.

The soldier moved off, and something in the way he gazed around tweaked Kai's suspicions. He waited to see which direction the soldier was heading, and then trailed him.

This was probably the dumbest thing he'd ever done, and quite clearly having nothing to do was already getting to him, but curiosity had grabbed hold of him, and he couldn't shake the feeling he needed to know more about the military guard who'd come up from Ilari with Cam McAllister.

Every now and then, the soldier would stop and seem to check out a shop or restaurant, before moving on again. Was he looking for someone, or just checking out commerce level to pass the time? When the soldier stopped outside of a burger joint, Kai paused, shifting closer to the window of the gift shop behind him as the soldier studied his surrounds with a perplexed look, almost as if he suspected he was being followed.

A couple of people moved into his line of vision, and Kai resisted the urge to change positions, instead waiting for the small group to move on. When they did, the front of the burger joint was clear, and the soldier nowhere to be seen.

Kai stepped out from the awning of the gift shop, scanning the thoroughfare, but couldn't see him anywhere. He hurried over to the fast food place and scanned the few people inside, and still nothing. That icy, troubled sensation surged higher through him, but he shook his head, pushing the feelings down.

The guy had probably just been meeting up with someone for an early lunch and here Kai was, following the man around like he was some sort of agent in a cliché TV show. If Sacha saw him now, she'd either laugh her ass off or check him into the *Knox*'s psyche annex for evaluation.

He wasn't going to escalate this farce by searching. Getting his finances organized was probably more important than trying to jog his memory. He checked his position, trying to work out where he'd ended up while following the soldier, and which direction he needed to go so he could find the BUE branch.

• • •

Sacha rubbed her aching back as she trudged into her apartment. After the excitement on flight deck this morning, she'd ended up even further behind today, and though she'd been on early shift—meaning she should have been able to come home around mid-afternoon—she'd ended up putting in an extra four hours, mostly of paperwork.

Kai was sitting in the same spot she'd seen him earlier this morning, except this time he was slouched back against the cushions with a beer in hand. Though she couldn't see the screen of the TV from here, it sounded like he was watching some kind of sports.

"Hey." He glanced up momentarily before returning his gaze to the screen. "Dinner is in the oven."

"Did you cook?" she asked, continuing on toward the kitchen, where a plate and wineglass were waiting on the bench for her.

"Nah, just ordered up from the Grill. I put it on your card. I didn't think you'd mind."

"The Grill two nights in a row, huh? Maybe I should just run a tab there for you." She took the containers out of the oven and found her favorite creamy pasta, with a side of warm crusty bread. As she poured a glass of wine, she tried not to think too closely about how nice it was to come home to company and dinner already waiting. Though she'd gotten used to being on her own, having someone around was definitely better.

But she couldn't get used to it. She gave herself a stern frown and stamped down the mushy feelings. Kai would only be here a few short nights, and then it would be back to a quiet apartment and organizing her own meals. And if that left her feeling deflated and hollow…? Well, eventually she'd get over it or learn to cope, like when Elliot had died, even if the result had been merely the shadow of an existence.

She forced away the dark thoughts and took her dinner and glass of wine over to sit on the armchair adjacent to Kai.

"How was your day?" They both asked at exactly the same moment.

She laughed as she stared down at her pasta. "Sorry, you go first."

"No, I'm sure you were busier. How are those fighter

pilots?"

She stabbed her fork into her dinner and shrugged one shoulder. "One only had minor injuries. He's already been discharged. The other was a little more serious, but he's stable and should recover."

Truthfully, she didn't feel like talking about work or her day. While it had been relatively normal, she felt more drained than usual. It probably had something to do with Kai coming back and the emotional stresses she kept refusing to think about. There'd be time to deal with herself later, after she was sure Kai was on the mend psychologically, as well as physically.

"What did you get up to?" she asked before shoveling a forkful of pasta into her mouth.

He leaned forward and gestured for the volume to lower on the TV, before looking back at her. "Not much. Caught up with Alpha before he disappeared into a briefing with Emmanuel, and then went to commerce level. Spent about two hours at the BUE branch, finding out what had happened to my accounts and whether I might be able to get my money back."

"So what happened to it all?" she got out between mouthfuls of food. As usual, the meal from the Knox Grill was delicious.

"Well, that's where things get confusing." He took a swig of beer, then set the bottle down. "Usually in the case of death, the funds are passed on to the next of kin, but I rang my parents, and they hadn't seen a cent of it. Same with my sister. The bank said if it hadn't gone to my family, then it might be in some holding fund, where unclaimed monies are put for seven years or something. They're going to follow it up for me."

"Well, that's good. It means you'll probably get it all back, right?"

He nodded, a shadow of distraction etching his features. "Could take days, or maybe weeks. They're going to let me know tomorrow if they find anything out."

"Did something else happen?"

He started to shake his head, lips pressed into a line. But then he picked up his beer to take another drink, and put the bottle down again, as though he were debating whether to tell her. She'd known him too long, and could easily tell when he had something on his mind. Whether or not he decided to share was another matter entirely.

"It's nothing," he said at last. "I just saw that soldier again, on commerce level. You know the one from yesterday that I thought I recognized, but couldn't place."

She dropped her focus to her plate as she finished up her meal. "Still can't remember?"

"No." Kai shifted forward, so he was sitting on the edge of the cushions. "But it's like something in my mind is telling me it's important, that I should know who this guy is."

He fisted his hands against his knees, gaze slicing away as his attention clearly turned inward, trying to solve this puzzle that seemed to have dug itself into his mind.

She reached out and wrapped her hand around his fist, regaining his attention.

"You know the more you try to think about it, the more it will elude you. Don't worry, it'll come when you least expect it, probably when you don't even care anymore."

"I know, but that doesn't make it any less frustrating. And there's something about him—" He shook his head and pulled back from her grasp, reaching over to grab his beer. "Never mind."

"What about him?" Sometimes, people suffering from PTSD focused almost obsessively on someone or something. It was a coping mechanism, so they didn't have to focus on their own issues. She'd been waiting for it almost every minute she'd been with him—the first sign of PTSD kicking in. There was no way he could have spent almost a year and half as a POW without experiencing some form of the disorder.

"This is going to sound nuts, even I know that, but my instincts are telling me there's something off about him. I just have no idea why. He was acting kind of suspicious when I saw him on commerce level this morning."

"Suspicious how?" She pitched her voice at an even tone, automatically slipping into doctor mode. Usually he would have called her on it, but he seemed too wrapped up in his own thoughts to notice.

"I don't know exactly. Just sort of wandering around, looking into all these shops but not going in, and then he just disappeared."

"I see."

Kai glanced up sharply at her, brows lowered over an indignant look. "I knew you'd laugh at me, or send me up for a psyche eval. And I know it's stupid, I told you that."

"I'm not laughing." Nope, she certainly wasn't. The psyche eval was probably closer to the mark, but since he was aware of how illogical his thoughts were, she wasn't that worried. "And I'm not going to check you into a padded cell at the psyche annex. This is perfectly normal. Your mind has just picked this particular soldier to focus on, so you're not constantly thinking about what happened to you."

The indignant expression deepened, with an edge of exasperation. "Thank you, Doctor Dalton, I didn't realize we were on the books right now."

"Sorry, Kai, but I told you when I offered my couch that I'd be monitoring your recovery."

He huffed out a sigh and sank back into the couch cushions, dragging both hands across his face. "So I should just forget about it, right? I probably won't see him again before he returns to the ground, and if I do, I'll just tell myself it's no big deal."

She sent him a short grin. "If all my patients were as smart and logical as you, I wouldn't need to work four extra hours like I did today."

"Then why are you still working, treating me like a patient?" He sat forward and reached down to grab her ankle. She'd kicked off her shoes at the door like she always did, and the sensation of his warm, callused fingers against her bare feet all but had her shuddering.

"Because technically you *are* my patient. And it's an occupational hazard. When you're a doctor, it's hard to ever really switch off."

She clamped her hands onto the armrests of the chair as Kai's thumb pressed into the ball of her foot and dragged down toward her heel. Pleasure rippled up her leg and a shiver followed in its wake. She could have groaned at the relief he was bringing her poor, abused feet. Instead she tugged, trying to reclaim the limb. "Thanks, but I think I'll go have a shower."

"Nuh-uh." He clamped his hand around her ankle to stop her from escaping. "I remember you always used to complain about your sore feet when you were an intern."

"Well now I'm used to it, I hardly even notice."

"Bull." He dug his thumb into a particularly sensitive spot and she had to bite her lip over a moan. Still, from the sharpening of his gaze, it appeared her pretense of being unaffected wasn't fooling anyone. "You're caring for me, sharing your home with me. I have to repay you in some way."

His voice had lowered a notch, and she tried to tell herself she was imagining the suggestive tone to his words. Yet, as she met his warm topaz gaze, the intensity of his regard closed around her, tempting her to forget her obligations and that there was anything else in the universe beyond the two of them.

She dragged in a deep, unsteady breath, hanging onto the last threads of her rapidly fraying composure. She'd been over and over why this was a bad idea. With Kai clearly displaying early signs of PTSD, now, more than ever, she had to be the one with a level head here, draw the line and commit to upholding it.

"We can't keep doing this." Her voice came out mostly even, with only the slightest hitch.

"What, foot massages?" His expression was all faked innocence.

This time when she tugged her foot, he let her go.

"You know what I mean. Yes, there are emotions and feelings between us, but it's too complicated. You can see that, right?"

"Yeah, I can see it." He pinned her in place with a look hot enough to melt every single resolve she'd armored herself with. "But I can also see how good it would be."

No. *No, no, no.* She started to get up, escape the only

way she could see getting through this with her resolutions intact. Until Kai came down on his knees in front of her, trapping her in the seat when he clamped both hands on the cushions on either side of her.

She swallowed, focusing on his eyes and not letting her gaze stray down to his mouth, not letting herself remember exactly how hot his kisses had been.

"Isn't that hurting your leg?"

He shrugged, and this close, she caught a glimpse of his biceps flexing at the movement.

"The dull ache I have is nothing to what I put up with in the last year. And at least I can actually bend it now, thanks to you." He leaned in closer. "Stop trying to distract me."

She flattened her hands against his chest to stop him getting any nearer. Her fingers tightened with the urge to caress the muscled expanse, instead of simply holding him at length.

"I'm serious. This is not going to happen between us."

"It will happen, because no matter how complicated it is between us, what I feel when I'm near you overrides everything else. Makes it simple and clear that this is exactly what I need. What we both need."

Her heart tripped over itself, and she swallowed against the sweet, rising heat within her. Grappling for the last of her control, she tried to set her features into a stern look, hoping he couldn't see her weakening resolve beneath.

"Maybe one day it will happen." Saying the words were harder than she'd imagined, but even if she could lie to her oldest friend, she had no doubt he'd see right through it. "But I'm telling you it's not going to happen tonight, or any time soon. Now if you don't mind, I need to go wash my hair."

His lips quirked up in a quick smile before he pushed back and returned to his seat. "All right then, go wash your hair, and take care of any other needs. Call out if you want some assistance — I'd be more than willing to help."

It took her a split second to catch his meaning, the smirk he sent her cementing the innuendo. A blush bloomed out of the heat she'd already been feeling, and she grabbed the cushion off the armchair to throw at him as she stood.

"Get your mind out of the gutter, Yang."

He caught the cushion against his chest. "Hey, it's not like I won't be doing the same thing later. Unless you're offering to help me."

His words pulled her up short and she glared over her shoulder at him.

"You better be joking about doing that in my shower!"

Great, she'd be in there washing her hair, and thinking about nothing but Kai with his hands on himself. And she didn't need to imagine some fantasy thanks to their recent shower together—she had every single detail of his body burned into her memory.

He didn't reply and, from the grin he sent her, she couldn't tell if he'd been joking or not. She chose to believe he was, otherwise when she got in the shower, she wouldn't need to turn the hot faucet on to make some steam; the cold water hitting her overheated body would do that all by itself.

Chapter Nine

Kai jerked awake, breath trapped in his lungs and heart hammering so hard, he swore it would give out on him any second. He glanced around, searching for Amos, praying for the gray light of dawn or the silvery-blue of the moon to be visible so he didn't strain his eyes against the pitch black of dead night. But his mind scrambled, not recognizing his surroundings for a long second.

"Kai."

Sacha. She was seated on the coffee table next to the couch, wearing a light robe, her hair in a tumbled mess, but her gaze sharp.

"It's okay, you're on the *Knox*, remember—?"

"Yeah." He pushed straighter, relieved as his drumming heart dropped a few paces. Unlike last time, when he'd had trouble shaking the thick web of the nightmare, his brain kicked into gear faster, clearing the confusion within moments.

Unfortunately it didn't take away the icy cold seeping through his soul, or the shock of his subconscious cooperating at last.

"It was him." He jerked to his feet, shoving the tangled blanket from around his hips and legs.

Sacha stood more slowly. "What was him?"

"The soldier." He grabbed her shoulders, the gratification of remembering ramming into a deluge of dark possibilities. "The soldier I recognized from the ground. He's CSS. He was one of the guards at the camp, but he was only around in the first two months or so, then we didn't see him again."

Because he'd infiltrated the UEF posing as a ground soldier? Or because he'd been a UEF operative inside the CSS Enlightening Camp? But then, why hadn't he reported that he and Amos were being held prisoner?

Sacha reached up and covered his hand with hers. "Slow down and explain it to me."

He took a short breath, forcing his racing thoughts into some semblance of order. "The soldier who accompanied Cam, who I've been trying to place. I saw him at the Enlightening Camp. He was one of the guards."

"Okay, how did you remember?" She didn't sound worried, just curious.

"The dream I just had. It was from before my leg got broken. He and another guard came into our cell one day and—"

"He was in your dream," she repeated, her voice calm and non-judgmental. Which meant she was definitely judging him and finding something wrong with his words.

"Yes, but it wasn't just a dream, it was a memory." His

words were clipped with impatience. He didn't need Sacha pulling her doctor crap on him, he needed her to listen. "Don't you get it? He's CSS, and he's infiltrated our ranks. Hell, Sacha, he's onboard the *Knox* right now. I knew he was up to something when I saw him yesterday. We have to warn Emmanuel—"

"Kai!" Sacha clamped her hands on either side of his jaw. "Calm down and think about this. We're not rushing off to tell Emmanuel anything without being absolutely certain."

He stepped out of her hold, disbelief slicing painfully through him. "I am certain. I remember clearly—"

"No, you had a bad dream." She crossed her arms, expression unforgiving. "I told you earlier tonight that often a person focuses on something as a coping mechanism. How do you know your mind didn't just put the face of that soldier onto a guard that maybe looked similar, because you've been obsessing so much about this?"

"I'm not obsessing, and I'm not crazy. I know it's him."

Her lack of belief in him cut to the bone, but he knew he was right about this. Every instinct told him his memory was real.

She shook her head. "I'm sorry, but I can't let you accuse some poor man of being CSS on nothing but the basis of a dream. And if you went to Emmanuel with this, he would tell you the same thing. Think about the ramifications, Kai. Do you want Emmanuel questioning your ability to return to duty?"

His lungs seized on the truth of that. Bad enough Sacha didn't believe him. He couldn't take even worse skepticism from Emmanuel, and no doubt the look of pity that would accompany it. Because the once-admirable Commander

Yang was now a crazy, paranoid son of a bitch. Yeah, that was one party he didn't want to play host to.

He took an unsteady step back and sat heavily on the couch, while some of his self-perceptions crashed down around him.

Sacha crouched in front of him. "It's okay. You don't need to worry about this, and by morning, neither of us will even think about it again. You had a nightmare and woke up confused. It happens to everyone, even people who haven't gone through the trauma you have."

He tore his gaze away from her compassionate expression, too close to sympathy for his comfort.

"I don't need a consult, Sacha. I just want to go back to sleep."

Yeah, like he'd get any more sleep tonight. But he didn't need her around offering her logical, clinical observations on his state of mind.

She stood with a low sigh. "Pushing me away isn't the answer."

He cut her a frustrated look. "Yeah? Well you seemed happy enough to push me away earlier tonight."

It'd been a low blow, and they both knew it. If he hadn't been feeling the sting of humiliation before, he sure as hell did now.

He kicked his legs up onto the couch and jerked the blanket off the floor. "Just leave me alone before I say something else we'll both regret. Unless you've changed your mind about what we were doing earlier…?"

Because feeling anything would be better, other than the dark, insecure confusion coursing through him.

Sacha didn't move away, but he refused to look up at

her. He could guess she had about a hundred other things she wanted to tell him, wanted to fix him as surely as she fixed every other patient under her care.

After a long moment, she left and, not long after, he heard the sound of her bedroom door closing.

Blowing out a long breath, he let his head drop back against the cushions and swallowed against the sudden press of loneliness. Maybe he shouldn't have been such an ass. Maybe he should have asked her to sit with him and chat, so long as they didn't talk about the dream or the soldier.

Instead, he had to lie here and try to ignore the ghosts of his captivity, with nothing else to keep him distracted.

• • •

Kai awoke to the trilling of the new comm Emmanuel had issued him. How and when he'd fallen back asleep, he had no idea, but his head throbbed and his eyes ached, like maybe he needed another few solid hours. Instead, he forced himself upright and groped for the comm sitting on the coffee table.

There was a message from Alpha, saying that he wasn't on-shift today, and was heading to the officers' gym if he wanted to join for a workout. He set the comm down again and rubbed his eyes, trying to clear the last haze of sleep from his mind.

"Sacha?" He checked her door, which stood wide open. The kitchen was empty, and he couldn't hear the shower running. A quick glimpse of the time told him she'd probably already gone to work.

Well, considering the way they'd left things last night,

that was probably a good thing. Though, it was also postponing the inevitable. They were going to have to talk about it at some stage, which brought him right back around to feeling the sting of her unconcealed disbelief.

In the clear light of day, the certainty that it hadn't been a dream, but a clear memory, returned and solidified. Okay, maybe he was damaged, both physically and psychologically from his time as a POW, and he would own that. But he was also the same guy Sacha had grown up with, and he was also Commander Yang, whose word had once been gospel. When he said he was convinced the soldier was the same guard from his confinement, couldn't she at least consider the possibility and not dismiss the idea out of hand?

With the CSS turning to offensives, that one of them had potentially infiltrated the UEF left him with a bad feeling churning low in his guts. Because if there was one, there would probably be more. There were too many deadly possibilities as to what CSS moles could do with their access.

There was no way he could get proof of his unfounded knowledge. Not unless he caught the soldier doing something suspicious or obviously counteractive to the UEF's efforts. But that would be next to impossible, short of following the man nonstop, which would only confirm Sacha's belief he was paranoid and obsessed.

Frustration pulsed through him, closely followed by a bitter helplessness. No matter what Sacha believed about his state of mind, Emmanuel needed to be made aware before the soldier made his move or found out he'd been compromised. Even if he risked ending up in the psyche annex for being paranoid and delusional, he had a responsibility to report his suspicions.

However, he couldn't rush out half-cocked—he needed something solid to back up his claim. This was going to take some serious consideration, so he pushed down the niggling problem as best he could while he scrounged up some breakfast and then showered. After he'd gotten dressed, there was another message on his phone from the BUE informing him that his money had been found, and would be returned to him in new accounts within the next forty-eight hours.

A small swell of relief ran through him. At least that took care of one issue. He could get closer to feeling like his old self once he had some funds at his disposal and could buy himself some basics.

He left Sacha's apartment feeling a little better about things, went up to the officers' gym, and found Alpha. The two of them quickly got into a routine, though it wasn't as vigorous as he would have liked. Before he'd been discharged from med-level, Macaulay had given him a lecture about doing too much. Usually he wouldn't have listened to Doctor Douche, but the threat of needing surgery on his bad leg kept him from really pushing himself. He could build himself back up over the days and weeks, until his body became used to the cathartic physical exertion again.

Alpha didn't try to talk about anything important while they worked out, it was mostly the usual guy stuff, which was a welcome relief. Even the problem of the CS Soldier hiding in their ranks left him alone for a while.

But once he and Alpha parted ways, Sacha and the conversation the night before consumed him. She hadn't deserved the brush-off he'd given her. Maybe he needed to go find her, clear the air. Except if he did find her, he wasn't quite sure what he'd end up doing with her.

The more time he spent with her, the harder it was to ignore the lust that had been on a constant, low simmer since the first day back on ship when he'd kissed her.

He wanted her in a way he'd never wanted another woman. Maybe it simply came down to a fact of denial—wanting what he couldn't have. Or maybe because it was *Sacha*, and he knew her well enough to believe going there with her would be amazing. She insisted things between them were complicated but, in his opinion, she was making it more problematical than it needed to be. The things he felt toward her were simple and pure. What was so wrong with wanting to get lost in that for a while with someone he trusted?

Sacha wasn't one to hold grudges. Still, she'd also want to talk about things, and he wasn't ready to go there yet, not until he'd be able to convince her he hadn't imagined recognizing the soldier. It was a simple matter of battle strategy.

In the meantime, he was going to make good on Cam McAllister's invitation to catch up while he was onboard the *Knox*. And if he happened to see a certain suspicious soldier in the meantime, then he'd just write that off as coincidence if she asked.

Chapter Ten

"If you stare any harder at that datapad; it's going to explode."

Sacha looked up from the charts she'd been reviewing to see Cassidy Willow standing in the doorway of her office.

"Something wrong?" Cass stepped farther into the room.

She set the datapad down on the desk and pushed at her hair, which somehow kept falling around her face, even though she'd tied it up earlier today.

"No, nothing more than the usual workload. I just haven't been sleeping very well lately." *For like the last year and a half.* Kai returning had only slightly disturbed the already disrupted sleep patterns she'd fallen into, but the constant emotional ups and downs were taking a toll.

Cass gave her a sympathetic look. "It doesn't help that you work such long hours. Give yourself a break once in a while."

"So I can get even further behind than I am most of the time?" She sent Cass a short smile, though there wasn't any humor behind the expression.

Cass walked around the desk and leaned over to press the power-down button on her datapad, before pulling her up from the chair.

"You've been running nonstop since Commander Yang came back, and I haven't seen you for more than two minutes at a time. We're going to get some lunch and spend at least an hour away from med-level."

A decent break and some food sounded great, but... "My patients—"

"Will be cared for by the fine medico staff currently on-shift, and will definitely still be here when you get back." Cass tugged her toward the office doorway. "Come on. I'll even call it my treat, if that'll seal the deal."

She took a moment to shrug out of her doctor's coat and leave it on the stand in her office. "You don't need to pay, you had me at *lunch*. I'm actually starving. I had half a cold coffee and a granola bar for breakfast."

Cass grimaced with a disgusted look. "Seriously, Sacha, you need a diet intervention."

"Remind me never to let you and Kai discuss that idea." Okay, maybe she should look after herself a little better. But she wasn't starving, and she did eat...usually at odd hours, sitting at her desk.

They bypassed the med-level cafeteria and headed to commerce level. At this time of day, there was quite a lunch crowd in the food sector. Cass led them toward the Knox Grill, but she hesitated outside the door.

"Do you want to eat somewhere else?" Cass asked, glancing at the other nearby cafés and other types of eateries.

"I've eaten here the last two days, but it's fine, there's

always something on the menu I want to have." There was no denying the Grill had the best food on the ship, which was why it was hard to get a table at peak meal times. Like now.

"We'll get takeaway and go eat somewhere else." Cass raised her voice to be heard over the loud chatter inside the busy restaurant.

They went up to the counter to order, and then stepped back to wait while their food was being prepared. Sacha scanned the crowd, her gaze snagging on Kai sitting at the bar, beer and plate of curly fries in front of him. He was grinning at something, and she shifted a little to see he was sitting next to Colonel McAllister.

Immediately, the tense conversation they'd had last night came back to her, and an unsettled feeling jolted through her. Did he still believe his nightmare to be a memory? Surely he wouldn't bring the possibility up with the colonel.

She glanced at Cass, who was watching a large screen across the room; some kind of news report that had a scrolling line of current headlines running across the bottom.

"Cass, I just saw someone I need to catch up with, I'll be back in a minute."

Sacha left her to navigate the crowd and head over to the bar. McAllister spotted her before Kai, sending her a polite nod.

Kai cut a look over his shoulder, and she might have been imagining it, but she could have sworn his gaze cooled when he saw her. Great. She was turning into the bad guy here when all she wanted to do was help him. Couldn't he see she was just ensuring he didn't commit career suicide with his unfounded allegations?

"Hi," she all but chirped. Fabulous, she sounded like an overly cheerful bimbo. "How are you both?"

McAllister murmured a polite response, but her focus was on Kai as he regarded her with something close to suspicion. He glanced at the colonel before standing.

"Cam, would you give us a moment?"

McAllister agreed, then picked up his beer and turned to someone sitting on his other side.

Kai wrapped his hand around her bicep and tugged her into motion, leading her toward a door that led off to the toilets and staff rooms. The door slid closed behind them, muffling the sharp noise of the restaurant to a dull murmur. Kai walked them into a room marked STAFF ONLY. It seemed to be some kind of office that also doubled as storage.

He let her go and then turned to face her. "What are you doing? Checking up on me?"

She crossed her arms, irritation flaring within her at his abrupt questions.

"No, actually. Cass and I came to get some lunch."

He scoffed and took a step closer to her. "Since when do you voluntarily leave med-level, or remember to eat for that matter?"

Her aggravation flamed higher. "Clearly I do eat just fine, considering I didn't waste away after Elliot was gone. And I think I should be the one asking the questions. It seems like more than a coincidence that you're having lunch with Colonel McAllister the morning after your dream."

Kai's expression was pure stubbornness, not giving anything away. "Cam invited me to catch up with him the other day. Are you telling me that reconnecting with my friends won't help my recovery?"

Damn, he had her with that one. And from the edge of smugness creeping into his features, he knew it, too.

"Don't be an ass, Kai. Whatever you're up to, it's not going to end well. You have to drop this and focus on what's important."

"Oh yeah? And is that your professional opinion?" He shifted closer to her again, and this time she took a step back to keep some distance between them. But he just kept coming, and when she bumped into the wall behind her, she had nowhere else to go, especially as his hands came up to brace on either side of her.

"There is one thing that is *very* important to me." His voice dropped lower, and she swallowed against the shiver rising through her. "I could show you just how important, if only you'd let me."

She clenched every muscle in her body, fighting any kind of reaction. He was like a faulty faucet—cold one second and hot the next. His push for a more intimate relationship with her was no different than his obsession with the soldier. Both were ways to avoid confronting what had happened to him. Besides, this little display was a blatant distraction technique, one she would not be fooled by.

Still, knowing that didn't help lessen the temptation to allow her walls to come down and let him do whatever he wanted with her. Each time she faced the lure of deepening their physical connection, it got harder to resist, her body humming with the need of the physical release he promised. He'd been right in what he'd said the night before. It seemed inevitable that eventually they would be together, but she wanted it to be under the right circumstances—because they cared deeply for each other and wanted to express those emotions, not as a Band-Aid to temporarily ease whatever turmoil was going on beneath the surface.

"I know what you're doing." Her voice came out steady enough, with only the slightest hitch to it. She dropped both hands on his shoulders to force him back a little.

"Yeah, I think it's pretty apparent myself." Despite her hold on him, he leaned closer. "Always so calm and collected. One of these days, you're going to lose control. I'm going to *make you* lose control."

Oh, god. Just the tenor of his low voice was almost enough to make her break. Her fingers contracted on his shoulders, digging into the muscles beneath his shirt. She gulped in a breath, and he closed the remaining distance between them. But he didn't kiss her. No, he brushed right by her mouth, his lips landing on the edge of her jaw, just below her ear. A shudder rocked her, and she only just managed to curb the moan wanting to slip free. His mouth moved up, over her lobe, breath spiraling warm against her skin.

"Tell me again, Sacha, why we can't have this between us?"

She opened her mouth, but no words came out, as if her brain had vacated the premises. Maybe just one kiss wouldn't hurt. After all, they'd shared a kiss or two already, and it hadn't really hurt anything…

Her comm vibrated in her pocket with a spell-breaking trill. She flattened herself against the wall, putting distance between them as she yanked the device out of her pocket.

Kai grabbed her wrist before she could check the screen. "Don't answer it. Not yet."

But the enthralling moment had been broken, and her senses had returned with an icy sting of self-recrimination.

She tugged her wrist from his hold, and he stepped back with a hard exhale, shoving a hand through his hair.

A message from Cass appeared on the screen, telling her their lunch was ready and asking where she'd gotten to. She slipped the comm back in her pocket and looked at Kai, his dark expression edged with a gleam of thwarted frustration.

"I have to go." She stepped away from the wall, brushing both hands over her clothes.

"One of these days, we're going to finish one of our conversations properly." He crossed his arms, spearing her with a resolute look.

She found herself nodding before she'd really thought about it. "Please, don't mention anything to McAllister about your suspicions until we've had a chance to discuss it further."

"You mean until you've convinced me it was all in my head?" His expression cooled. "I'm not a moron, Sacha. I never planned on saying anything to Cam today. I really did just want to catch up with the guy."

"Good. That's good." She nodded again, but then felt a bit silly. For a long moment they stared at each other.

She moved toward the door. "I'll see you tonight."

He murmured a good-bye, and she ducked out, breathing easier once she was no longer in the same room with his too-tempting presence.

• • •

Sacha forced herself not to pause before stepping through the door into her apartment. Kai had been on her mind all afternoon, her thoughts swinging like a pendulum from her worry about whether he'd follow through on his suspicions over the soldier, to the words that had branded themselves into her mind… *One of these days, you're going to lose control. I'm going to make you lose control.*

Kai obviously didn't agree with her position that any deep emotional connection between them would end in disaster and possibly compromise his recovery. And, unfortunately, her own desires burning against a weakening resolve, fostered by the wretched loneliness of the past year, were only making things worse.

Spending hours alone in her apartment with him seemed like a bad idea, especially when her thoughts kept circling back around to the hot, easy temptation of him. But what else was she going to do with herself?

She'd considered finding an empty cot in a quiet corner on med-level and bunking down there for the night, but she didn't want to leave Kai to his own devices, and needed to be there if he had another nightmare. Plus, if she didn't come home tonight after the moment between them at the Grill, he'd totally call her for a coward…and he'd be right.

However, her trepidation over coming home turned out to be pointless, as inside she found her apartment cool, dark, and obviously empty. As some tension drained from her shoulders, she went through the usual routine of kicking off her shoes, emptying her pockets, and shrugging out of her jacket.

As the lights came on, she adjusted the environmentals and then headed into the kitchen to pour herself a glass of red wine and contemplate what kind of simple meal she could put together, because eating from the Grill twice in one day and three nights in a row just didn't seem right. She had just decided on a pasta dish when the door to the apartment slid open, and Kai walked in.

Glancing up, the *hello* she'd intended to say got lost as she took in the sight of him in his UEF uniform.

If this meant he'd gotten his old position back, she should have been elated for him, instead an acid surge of trepidation swelled within her. Was this it? Had his future been decided and he was about to tell her he'd shortly be leaving the *Knox* for good?

She took a quick sip of wine to clear her throat. "Looks like you've been busy since I saw you at lunch."

He shrugged and slid the neatly pressed jacket off his shoulders to hang next to hers on the coat stand, then tilted his chin up to tug at his tie and flick open the top fastening of his shirt.

"Emmanuel contacted me not long after you left and I ended up spending the afternoon in the command center. Just been taking care of some formalities." He walked forward, glancing at her glass of wine as he joined her in the small kitchen. "Got another one of those somewhere?"

She turned away from him to fetch a glass from the cupboard. "So, does this mean...?" The words trailed off, because apparently the apprehensive tightening in her throat made it too hard to voice her thoughts.

"That I've been given a posting? No. At least, not that I know of yet. They're not going to make a quick decision. You know how the UEF love their bureaucratic BS. However, they've assured me that I'll still play an important role, and..." He reached out and took the glass of wine she'd poured, cutting an uncertain glance in her direction.

"And?" That look he was giving her made the next breath

catch in her chest.

"And, if I don't want to wait for a decision, if I want to cede my place on the *Valiant Knox*, there's a vice commodore position back on Earth."

Vice commodore? Technically, it was a promotion. Except everyone knew segueing into a commodore role meant it was time to be put out to pasture.

"But you're not even thirty-five yet." She clamped her lips closed after the words blurted out.

Kai gave a cynical laugh. "Exactly what I thought."

He shook his head slightly, before taking a short sip of wine.

Sacha swallowed down a few more impulsive words, considering the right thing to say. "I mean, it's a promotion, and being the youngest person to ever make vice commodore would have its perks, right?"

Except he'd be on Earth, light-years away in an entirely different system. It would be years before they saw each other again. If ever. Trips to Earth weren't cheap, and her contract with the UEF to serve onboard the *Valiant Knox* didn't exactly come with the bonus of six-month holidays.

"It would have its advantages." He turned an absent stare to the wineglass in his hands and then set it down on the bench.

"So you're considering it?" The tightening in her throat turned into a lump. He couldn't do it, couldn't leave her when she'd just gotten him back—

She ruthlessly shut down the desperate line of thinking. This shouldn't be about what she wanted or needed, it had to come down to what was right for Kai. Maybe staying on the *Valiant Knox*—so close to the place he'd spent almost eighteen months living in hell—wouldn't be the best situation for his recovery. A fresh start and a new role might be the best thing he could do for himself in moving forward with his life.

He scrubbed a hand over his hair. "I don't know. They only just suggested it. I need time to think."

She dropped her gaze from him. "Okay, then. What do you feel like for dinner? I was thinking pasta—"

"Sacha." His hands landed on her shoulders. "I'm not going to make any decision without talking to you first."

"Why?" She looked up at him, setting her expression into determined detachment.

A short smile quirked up his lips. "You really going to ask that question? Stand here and play dumb?"

"I can give you my professional opinion about what each option would mean for your recovery—"

He yanked her forward, his mouth catching hers and cutting off the words.

"I don't want you to play doctor now," he said against her lips. "I just want you, Sacha, the girl I met when I was sixteen, the friend who's known me longer than anyone else on this entire ship, the woman whose memory got me through the darkest nights in that damn prison."

Before she could even think of replying, before she'd hardly gasped in a breath, Kai pressed his lips to hers again, the kiss demanding and wholly unapologetic. He made it plainly obvious what he wanted from her, and this time, she got the sense he wouldn't let anything stop or slow him down.

For half a second she groped for all the reasons why this was a bad idea, but couldn't come up with a single one. With

Kai pulling her up against the lean hardness of his body, his mouth and tongue coaxing her into a place of heated magic and liquid euphoria, she didn't know why in hell she'd been resisting.

Kai's fingers trailed from her shoulders, across her upper chest to the fastenings of her shirt. He started shuffling her back, even as he began yanking at material, pulling her shirt free from her pants and parting the sides to slip his hands along her ribs. With shivers rippling over her skin from every place his callused fingers touched her, she tugged at his clothes hastily in return, freeing the fastenings until she could push the shirt clean off his shoulders.

The lower padding of the couch bumped into her legs. Kai grabbed her up, and she wrapped her legs around his waist as he tilted her down, setting her on the cushions and then coming down on top of her.

A wild spark ignited, and desperation edged into the movements between them, as though the very universe around them would go down in flames if they didn't come together right this moment, if they didn't press into each other and fall out of control in equal measure.

With impatience, she squirmed to pull her pants off, needing the hard length of him inside her, needing everything she knew he could give her. Like breathing, it had become necessary they join, that he eased the desolate brittleness that had started crystallizing inside her ever since the day she'd heard he'd gone missing.

At last naked, she sighed in anticipation and relief, wrapping her legs around his lean waist again. Kai moved back to look down at her, unbuckling his belt and flicking open the top clasp of his pants. With a slow movement, he eased back down, his fingers sliding into her hair and then tilting her head back slightly.

His topaz eyes burned gold as he stared down at her. The possessive, wild gleam in his gaze made her heart skip a few beats and in that moment, she could see how much this meant to him. This was no simple moment when he'd lost his head. No. For him, it seemed this was a commitment. An unspoken agreement that what they were doing went far deeper than physical need.

A cold wash of uncertainty took the edge of her reckless desire, the gravity of what they were about to do impacting squarely in the middle of her chest with unforgiving force. But then his erection came up against her very center, hot and heavy and so very right, and it was all she could do to breathe as he started the slow push to set himself inside her.

Chapter Eleven

Kai swallowed over the tightness in his throat as he pushed his erection against the slick, wet heat of Sacha. Bare vulnerability gleamed in her eyes as she gazed up at him. The sight filled his chest with burgeoning feeling and warmed places inside him he'd thought would remain cold forever.

This, right here, this woman—his closest friend whose memory had been his very lifeline in hell—*this* was his salvation.

He tightened his hold on Sacha's waist and pressed his hips forward, sliding himself into her by torturous, gradual degrees, when his instincts were hammering at him to plunge recklessly and take her like a man possessed.

Sacha's eyes slid closed and the low moan she made as he eased his cock all the way inside her made his insides clench. His heart rate jacked, his pulse skittered, and fine tingles started breaking out over his skin. This wasn't going to be a long, drawn out seduction. It was all he could do in that second not to lose his head and come on a single re-strained thrust.

She tilted her hips up toward him, undulating in a sensuous rhythm that made sweat bloom over his lower back. With hardly any control or coordination, he retreated and lunged forward in a short stroke. She groaned again and he closed his mouth over hers with abandoned temerity. When her tongue slid against his, he shuddered all over and thrust beyond any hope of reining things in. She was so wet, so hot, and it seemed like a lifetime since he'd felt anything like this.

As a thunder started vibrating deep within him, roaring upward and outward, Sacha cried out and arched beneath him. Her short nails dug into his shoulders and then everything erupted into pure blinding sensation. His lungs seized and heart stuttered as a tidal wave of ecstasy rolled through him and washed everything from its path.

Kai dragged in a ragged breath and collapsed half on top of her, his arms set with a light tremble. Every part of him felt a relieved cleanness. Almost like being reborn. Just as she had tidied him up in the wash facilities in his med-lab room the first night he'd returned, tonight she'd shown him that the grimy, soiled parts of the CSS prison within him could be purified from his heart. They'd never be wiped from his memories, but at least the recollections wouldn't be able to hurt him any longer.

She released a low breath, a contented sound that made his inside swell with stupid pride, as her fingers ruffled through his hair.

He lifted his head to look up at her. "Do I have to stay on the uncomfortable couch tonight, or can I come to bed with you?"

She laughed and swiped her tangled hair from her fore-head. "You would say something like that right after…" Color darkened her cheeks after the words trailed off.

"Having sex? *Great* sex? Making love? You can say it, can't you?"

The color deepened, but her laugh wasn't self-conscious. "Fine, after making love. I wouldn't put it past you to seduce me just so you didn't have to sleep here."

He frowned at her, but kept the expression light. "I would never do any such thing."

"Oh yeah? Cindy Kent ring any bells?"

He flinched. "Heard about that one, huh? In my defense, I was pretty drunk and having a bed to sleep in wasn't the only reason I—"

Sacha slapped her hands over her ears and glared. "I don't want to hear it, not after…" She made a kind of waving motion between them. "Not when we're like this."

He hugged her closer, hiding a grin. Joking around with her brought back happy memories, though it still gave him a weird feeling of disconnection, like the life they spoke of had happened to someone else.

She groaned and pushed at his shoulder. "Look at the time, I have to get some dinner and get to bed or I'll be dead on my feet tomorrow. I've got another early start."

He leaned back, but only far enough to catch her mouth in a deep, tender kiss. The urge to say something like "thank you" tumbled to his lips, but he pulled back on the notion. No doubt she'd take his platitude the wrong way and it would probably sound even more stupid out loud than it did in his head. The words *I love you* followed closely behind and he broke the kiss to look down at her.

Jesus god, he loved her. Not that he was surprised. He'd always loved her as a friend and maybe something a little more than that. But now the emotion infused every cell inside him. He was hers. Totally. Undeniably. Though she didn't realize yet and he couldn't quite bring himself to tell her. Things were so very new and precarious, he couldn't even consider he might mess this up with one ill-thought-out phrase.

She smiled up at him, her hand gentle on the side of his face. "Don't look so serious, you can share my bed. But I need to sleep, so if you even think of trying anything, I'll bust you back down to the couch so fast, you'll get friction burns."

He shook his head as he climbed off her and then helped her up. "You always did lay things out straight."

She shrugged, beautiful and sensual in the soft light, and totally comfortable with her nudity. "That way it helps avoid any misunderstandings."

Sacha disappeared into her bedroom, while Kai went to retrieve the clothes they'd littered all over the place. By the time he found his pants and shirt, she'd returned in sweat pants and a light T-shirt, combing out her hair. She sent him a sweet smile and made her way to the kitchen, picking up her wineglass and then pulling out various items to make dinner.

The evening went by with easy contentment, and before he knew it, Kai was trailing Sacha into her bedroom. As she flipped down the blankets, he paused, studying her face for any hint of hesitation or second thoughts. What had happened on the couch earlier had been spontaneous and impulsive, but making the conscious decision for him to join her in the bed she'd once shared with Elliot was a whole other matter.

However, she appeared totally at ease, so he stepped farther into the room before she noticed his loitering and thought *he* was the one with the issue. Yeah, he had issues, but none of them had anything to do with Sacha and the new wealth of feelings coursing through him.

He stripped down to his boxer-briefs and then settled under the blankets next to her, wrapping his arms around her to keep her close. The lights above them blinked out, leaving the room in deep darkness, apart from the muted glow from the numbers of the clock next to the bed.

Sacha snuggled against him and he felt her relax in his hold. He couldn't help but run light, stroking caresses along the warm, bare skin of her arm. She made a contented noise but then slapped at his hand.

"Hey, remember earlier when I said sleeping only? The couch threat is very close to becoming a reality."

Before she could struggle out of his grasp, he rolled them and set himself on top of her. "I'd like to see you try."

He lowered his lips to taste her skin, just under her jaw, using his other senses to explore her since he couldn't see anything in the dark.

She sighed his name and arched beneath him, making a quiet laugh rumble up from within him. There was plenty of time for sleep later.

· · ·

Sacha closed her eyes and opened up her other senses—the heated feel of Kai's skin against her, the deliciously masculine smell of him surrounding her, the uneven catch to his breathing as his hands slid over her. In the dark, all of these things became magnified.

You'll be a wreck tomorrow if you don't get some sleep. The weak voice in her head sounded half-hearted at best, especially as he tugged up her T-shirt and closed his mouth over a hardened nipple, the graze of his teeth catching her by surprise, shooting sparks of pleasure through her body.

When Kai had joined himself with her before, when they'd wrapped together and gotten lost in a thrall of ecstasy, she felt as though they'd forged a new connection, one they'd never had before. For him, this wasn't just some cheap thrill or a surrender to base urges. She could see that in each moment he spent with her, the layers of the CSS prison shell were falling away to reveal...not Kai as she'd known him exactly. But a new man. A stronger man, even if he might not be able to see it himself.

He moved his mouth over to her other nipple, biting down a little harder this time, shattering any coherent thoughts she'd been clinging to. She gasped at the shooting pleasure, causing him to repeat the action, pinching the other nipple with his fingers until he had her squirming.

His hand slid down over her stomach, under the elastic band of her pants and when his fingers reached her pubic bone, she moaned in sheer relief for the fact he was going to do something about the tension he'd been winding up within her. She let her thighs fall open as his hand cupped her sex. Wanting more, she undulated against his palm, and was rewarded with a finger sliding inside her. But it wasn't enough, she needed more, needed him to build her up and then set her free.

His mouth moved from her breast and slid up the length of her neck until he found her mouth. And then a second finger joined the first, thrusting deep inside, right where she needed. He set a languid rhythm, one that she enjoyed as much as she loathed. She wanted him faster, harder, to send her over the edge into a rippling orgasm. Yet each stroke was so lusciously measured, so carefully constrained. He knew exactly how to play her. And she was enjoying the exquisite torture of every moment.

By slow degrees, he increased the pressure and speed until the build up within her started becoming critical. And then he withdrew. She cried out at the loss of his clever fingers, but in another second, her pants were gone and the head of his erection pressed into her. She relaxed back with a relieved breath. He rolled her, the world tilting in the darkness, before she found herself on top of him. With a satisfied grin she couldn't see, she braced her hands against his chest and lowered herself onto his hard shaft. The relief and temptation for more pulsed through her. As she slid against him, he anchored his hands on her hips, fingers tight in her flesh.

"Sacha—" Her name in the darkness, inflected in a way only Kai ever did, made her heart triple-beat in her chest. With that simple word, she shattered, grinding down against him as the orgasm started deep within her and radiated outward like warm sunshine.

Kai shuddered underneath her and she felt him coming deep inside her. And she'd never felt more satisfied than she did right in that moment.

Chapter Twelve

Sacha dropped into the chair behind her small desk and took a moment to rub her dry, bleary eyes. After getting less sleep than she'd needed the night before, she felt about as bad as she expected.

No, actually she felt worse.

Last night… A small shiver rippled through her, even as a spike of guilt rammed right through the middle of her chest. Last night, in the heat of the moment with Kai, making love had seemed like a great idea, had been the only outcome she could see from the emotion that had been building between them since his return. It had been a reaffirmation that he'd really returned, a moment of living in the most literal sense after all those dark days she'd dealt with the lonely, soul-crushing bleakness of death.

Even this morning, she'd woken up feeling too satisfied, and gotten ready for her shift in a warm glow of ignorant contentment, leaving Kai still sleeping in her bed.

But then she'd stepped out of her apartment and into reality, where yes, she had slept with the guy who was technically her patient, whose mental and physical wellbeing should have been put far above her own desires.

Sure, he'd obviously been a more-than-willing participant. But that hadn't stemmed the rising, complicated guilt, building as the day wore on, and she thought more closely about what she had done. She'd broken one of the most sacred rules as a doctor—taken advantage of someone in an emotionally vulnerable state, leading him into thinking there was something between them when there couldn't be.

He should have been concentrating on his recovery, and now he would no doubt focus even more intently on her, instead of dealing with the fallout from being in that CSS prison. He'd straight out told her that he'd hung on to the memory of her in order to survive. It wasn't a stretch of the imagination to consider he'd hang on to the promise of a relationship to avoid facing the scars of his captivity.

She'd treated so many returned prisoners over the years, knew all the pitfalls and mechanisms the psyche could put up to deal with trauma, yet she'd had a moment of selfish weakness with Kai, the results of which could be deep and far-reaching.

When he'd come to med-level to share lunch with her, she'd gotten one of the nurses to tell him she was too busy today. Now there were only a handful of things left for her to do before she ended her shift to face Kai and who-knew-what kind of fallout from the night before.

She frowned as she pulled a datapad out of the top drawer before clicking it into place, just above the inset touch-screen keyboard on the surface of the desk. As she waited for her files to load, she propped her elbow on the desk and set her heavy head against her palm.

A knock brought her attention up. Macaulay stood in the doorway, one hand braced against the doorjamb.

"The reports for Commander Yang have been amalgamated into one file. I'm available to confer if you want a second pair of eyes on it."

An automatic refusal landed on her tongue, but she swallowed down the words as doubt, and another lance of guilt, ran through her. Usually the higher ranking doctors each handled the ongoing care of POW cases alone, and technically Kai had been her patient. Except she'd gone and let their relationship sink into very personal realms. What if her emotions got in the way and she missed some critical piece of information? She'd probably already done more than enough damage last night; instead she had to do everything in her power to make sure he got the first-class treatment he needed and deserved.

"Actually, I was just about to review my case files, and I would appreciate a back up on Commander Yang's situation. There're going to be a lot of people watching his recovery very closely, and if there are two doctors signing off on everything, the findings will be less likely to be called into question."

Macaulay nodded and stepped into her office. "Good point. Might as well beat the bureaucrats at their own game."

As she brought up Kai's file, he sat in the chair on the opposite side of her desk.

"Just give me a minute to read the psychologist's report, and then we'll discuss care options for him." She tabbed through until she found the report, but got distracted by

Macaulay shifting in his seat. She brought her head up to see the other doctor had a troubled expression on his face. "Something wrong?"

"I had an ulterior motive for coming to speak with you."

She sat back from the datapad, a barbed stream of guilt and trepidation rushing through her. Had Macaulay somehow found out about—? But no, that would be impossible. She and Kai were literally the only two people who knew what had happened the night before.

"So, spit it out, you know how I prefer to have things laid out straight."

Macaulay rubbed a hand over his jaw. "It's just that I heard Commander Yang is still staying with you."

A prickly wall of defense sprung up within her as her shoulders tensed, making her neck ache. "He didn't have anywhere else to stay—"

Macaulay held up a hand. "I don't have a problem with it, Sacha. I know you and Commander Yang were friends long before either of you started serving on the *Valiant Knox*. But you can't tell me there's not a conflict of interest here. Besides that, you know that the next few weeks are going to be critical for Yang's successful recovery. I just want to state that I think you need to make a choice. You're either acting as his doctor and keeping a professional distance, or you're there as his friend, in which case, you can't be the one overseeing his continued care. And if you do decide to continue from here out as his friend, then we both know that there are certain emotional landmines you need to avoid."

Sacha cut her gaze away from him, wrapping her hands around the armrests of the chair until her knuckles started aching.

Damn it. He was right. *God*, she shouldn't have slept with Kai last night. She'd gone and stepped on about twenty of those emotional landmines in a few short hours.

Emotionally, Kai was vulnerable and fragile, though he'd never admit to it. Things would get harder for him before they got better.

Are you ten kinds of idiot or what, Dalton?

She couldn't be his friend, she didn't know how, and last night had only proven that. Where her feelings and Kai were concerned, she obviously had self-control issues. Which meant if she truly wanted to help him get through the darkest time in his life, then she couldn't give him anything except her professional care, until he was physically and emotionally in the process of moving on.

"You're right, Macaulay. I want to make sure Commander Yang has the best chance of getting past his time as a POW with as little fallout from PTSD as possible."

"Good, I had a feeling you'd say that." He stood. "I've got a surgery. Take your time reading the reports, and we'll confer in the morning."

She murmured a good-bye as he left her office, and she turned her attention to Kai's file. A dull ache throbbed in the middle of her chest in time with the sluggish beat of her heart. Part of her hated the realization she'd come to, and part of her really hated the weakness that had led her into this trouble in the first place.

She would do whatever it took to get Kai through the coming weeks and months, even if she had to hurt him in the process by detaching.

• • •

Something wasn't right. Kai set down the knife he'd been using to chop the tomatoes and ran a check over the ingredients laid out across Sacha's bench. Something was missing, but he couldn't work out what. And stupidly, he'd taken far longer cutting up the vegetables than he needed to, because he couldn't remember exactly what order to cook everything.

He stepped back from the bench and dragged a hand over his face, forcing his thoughts to slow and settle. His mind was racing, too many snatches of random things careening around in his head. Much more of that, and it felt like his mind was about to go into meltdown. All over trying to cook a simple goddamn meal.

Before he'd been captured, he'd enjoyed cooking, and this wasn't the first time he'd prepared a meal in this kitchen. Although, in the past it'd usually been with Elliot, trying to pass on some culinary skills to his friend, who could hardly cook eggs without burning something.

Making a nice meal for Sacha had seemed like the perfect way to greet her when she got home from her shift on med-level, but somewhere around the onions, it'd started turning into a disaster.

A tremor shot through his arms, down to his hands, and he braced his clenched fists against the edge of the bench, blowing out a long breath.

He should be able to do this with his eyes closed; this recipe had been one of his favorites, the process of making it stamped into his subconscious. So why the hell was it so hard? How could he have forgotten something so simple?

The tremor in his arms spilled into his shoulders and tripped down his spine, causing a cold sweat to bloom over his skin. The jumble of his thoughts got louder, faster, more intense, flashes of images surfacing from the shadows of his mind.

His heart thumped hard, and his next lungful of air came too short. What the hell was this? Some kind of panic attack? He clenched his fists harder, locking down every muscle in his body. *No*. This was not happening. He refused to give any more energy to the CSS and their goddamn Enlightening Camp. He'd escaped. It was in the past. He had better things to do with his life than dwell on his time there.

Except a tidal wave of guilt followed in the wake of his momentary stubborn determination to move on. Yeah, he'd escaped, but Amos had been there with him every day. And Amos hadn't escaped. Amos was still there. Confusion sloshed through his mind, numbing some of the roiling emotions. Amos was still there, but he was dead. Blood filled his vision. Cold seeped through his veins, along with pain and sickness. And he was hacking that alloy rod free from a dead friend's arm, and then the CSS guards were falling, and the blood crept closer.

Something clamped onto his shoulder and he spun with a guttural shout of fury. He had to escape. Escape or die. He refused to spend another day in that cesspool of misery and torment.

He slammed his attacker up against the wall, gasping for his last breath, because this CS Soldier would kill him too easily—

"Kai. *Kai!*"

He shook his head, the sweat dripping down his forehead stinging in his eyes. The scent of summer acacia laced his next breath, jamming him back into reality, where he was standing in Sacha's kitchen, with her shoved up against the wall—

Jesus, he had a blade at her throat. His hand went weak at the sight, and the knife he'd been using to cut up the vegetables clattered to the floor in the heavy silence.

"Oh, god." He stumbled back a step, but his bad knee gave out and he slipped down to the floor next to the bench. Nausea churned his guts, sending bile burning up the back of his throat. He'd almost killed her, almost shoved a knife into Sacha's throat. What the hell was wrong with him?

"Kai, it's all right, we're fine. Just breathe." She crouched down in front of him, but he couldn't look directly at her, his brain was still fritzing like a ship in a tailspin, about to crash into oblivion.

"I'm sorry." His voice grated out thick and awkward.

"It's okay, I shouldn't have come up behind you, but I thought you'd heard me come in. It's not your fault. Just take a minute to get your bearings."

He squeezed his eyes shut, an illogical surge of anger burning away some of the confusion. Why did she have to be so damn understanding? Couldn't she see how close he'd come to losing it right then? If he'd hurt her—

His chest constricted, cutting off his ragged breathing and putting pressure on his heart, until a pulsing ache shuddered through his entire body. He yanked at the collar of his shirt.

"You're having a panic attack, Kai, so you need to breathe deeply, okay?"

He looked up, finding her smoky blue gaze fixed on him with concerned intent.

"I'm not having a goddamn panic attack, so stop telling me to breathe."

Her lips twitched as she reached out to grasp his hand. "Okay, you're not having a panic attack."

At her touch, relief broke up the hard sensations tearing through him. On blind instinct alone, he wrapped his arms around her, dragging her closer to bury his face in her neck.

Now he could breathe. The hard pounding of his heart slowed, and sweet lassitude chased the tension out of his muscles.

"I'm sorry," he murmured against the sweet-scented skin of her neck. This time his words had more substance. "That shouldn't have happened. I'll be more careful next time."

She eased back from him, but he tightened his grip on her, since even that slight movement let some of the apprehension return. He couldn't let her go yet, not until he'd gotten a handle on whatever *that* had been. This woman was the balm to his soul, making the tattered edges easier to hold together.

"It's not about being careful, Kai. And what happened just now was no one's fault. PTSD is a complex—"

"I don't have PTSD." As soon as he snapped the words, he heard how stupid they sounded.

She raised an eyebrow at him. "Is that your professional opinion, Commander Yang?"

He closed his eyes for a long moment, huffing out a deep sigh. "I'm sorry, I don't have experience with this sort of thing. I mean, I read the reports of other soldiers under my command who suffered from it, but I never thought—"

"No one ever thinks it's going to happen to them, until it happens to them. And then they're left with no idea of how to pick up the pieces."

He breathed in slowly, trying to get his mind to accept

what his body already knew. Stubborn pride wouldn't help him heal. PTSD… It could haunt him for years if he didn't accept what his time as a POW had done to him. "So how do I beat this?"

Sacha moved back out of his hold and stood. "Well, for a start, we can finish cooking dinner."

Kai levered himself up using the kitchen bench, tentative when he put his weight back on his bad leg, but thankfully, it held, returning to the dull ache he'd tolerated since they'd taken the BMC off him.

The urge to feel her against him raked through him like the deepest craving. Dinner could wait, because food wasn't the sustenance his body and soul required in that moment.

She walked over and picked up the knife, then dropped it into the sink. A cold flush made icicles prickle beneath his skin, but he refocused on the desire he'd been feeling a moment ago. *Sacha.* He just needed her, needed to find salvation in her.

As she stepped closer to him, probably to inspect his over-chopped vegetables, he hooked an arm around her waist, tugging her up against him.

"Never mind dinner, we'll finish up later, or call for some takeout."

She braced her hands against his chest, her expression guarded. That wasn't what he wanted. He needed to see the same soul-deep emotion they'd shared last night in her gaze.

He lowered his head, but she ducked his kiss, sending his heart rate plummeting. And when she twisted out of his grasp…the cold within him returned, freezing his blood in his veins.

"Kai, we need to talk." Her words were heavy with regret,

tinged with ominous sobriety.

"Talking isn't what we need." His response didn't sound quite as flippant as he'd wanted it to… Maybe she hadn't noticed the hint of desperation. With a short step, he tried to close the distance between them once more, but Sacha dodged his movements.

"I'm serious, Kai, and I mean that as your doctor, not as a friend."

He stepped back to brace himself against the bench, feeling too unsteady. This wasn't how he'd planned the night to unfold; everything was literally falling apart around him. "Okay, so let's talk, because I thought I'd be entertaining Sacha tonight, not Doctor Dalton."

She sent him an unimpressed frown before turning to the coldstore and retrieving a bottle of white wine. "I'm going to need this first."

He watched as she poured a glass, but halted her from getting a second glass out for him. His brain already felt like slush, the last thing he needed was to add alcohol to that.

She pushed a few loose tendrils of hair back, before taking a gulp from her wineglass. She set the drink back down on the bench and then turned to him with a decisive movement.

"I've tried to think of a hundred different ways to start this conversation, and none of them seem right. So, I just want you to listen and try to understand."

He nodded and swallowed, because when a conversation started out like that, it never boded well. However, he could guess where she was going with this. She felt guilty over last night. Whether the ghost of Elliot still stood between them, or something else had sent her into a deep hole of doubt, well, he'd find some way to get them around it. Because he needed her like he'd never needed another person. He'd been his own man since he'd left home at twelve to board at the pre-mil training school. Yet in this second, he couldn't imagine how he would get through the next hour without her, let alone the next day, or week, or month.

She crossed her arms as she regarded him. "Last night was amazing and wonderful. I wouldn't change it for anything. But it shouldn't have happened. I shouldn't have let it happen."

"It takes two. Don't forget I'm half of the responsible party." He sent her a strained smile, trying to keep the mood light, but the panic was pushing at the edges of his control, mixing with a subtle sense of helplessness that blended perfectly to create acidic anger. "Whatever reason you think it shouldn't have happened, you're wrong. This thing between us, *you*, it's exactly what I need right now."

"No it's not." She closed her hand around the stem of the wineglass, but didn't pick it up, her gaze focused downward. "I'm sorry, because allowing that to happen has confused things between us. I'm your doctor, the person in charge of your ongoing care as a former POW. You know as well as I do how many rules we broke by being together last night."

The blending anger started burning hotter within him. "Screw the rules. Get someone else assigned to my case. I don't need you to be my doctor; I need you to be my friend. More than my friend. I don't know what that makes us, but what happened between us last night was right. It made me forget. I need to be able to lose myself in you. It's the only way I can get through this."

She brought her head up, a shadow of sadness and

self-recrimination in her gaze. "What you're telling me only confirms my decision. Using me as a distraction is not a healthy way of recovering, and I won't let you do it. Facing what happened to you in the CSS camp is almost going to be harder than when you lived through it. And while I'm here for you—I'll *always* be here for you—I can't, in good conscience, let you use me as a crutch."

Every word she said hammered into his chest, like a nail sunk one strike at a time. "I'm not trying to use you as a crutch. Is it so wrong that I care about you? Don't tell me you didn't feel anything last night."

Her expression tensed. "Of course I care."

Kai rubbed the back of his neck where his muscles were aching. "I know you're only trying to do what you think is best for me, but don't I get a say? What if this is exactly what I need?"

She shook her head and dropped her gaze again. "I'm sorry. It's just not."

"So that's it, then?" The anger he'd been holding in slipped a notch, getting closer to the surface of his calm. "You decide how I'm going to get through this, and that's the end of the story?"

"I've overseen the care of more than a few POWs, so yes, I'm telling you in my professional opinion, this is how it's going to be. At least until you've started making progress on moving past everything."

"So I'm just supposed to wait around like a lapdog until Doctor Dalton decides I'm well enough to be in her bed again. How fortunate for me." Heat throbbed in his chest and he turned to stare at the vegetables he'd been chopping because he couldn't look at Sacha any longer; it hurt too damn much. How could she do this to him right when he needed her the most?

He'd thought they'd shared something deep, something important. Obviously he'd been wrong, because if she felt even half of what he felt for her, then she wouldn't have been standing here calmly telling him they couldn't be together, because the idea would be tearing her apart.

Just like it was ripping through him, leaving a blackened trail of fury in its wake.

"It's not like that." She took half a step toward him. "Please believe that I *am* doing this for you, because you're the most important thing to me—"

"Don't try to tell me now how much you care!" The black rage within him turned white-hot. His fist closed around the bottle of wine, and with a single, sharp movement, he'd smashed the glass into a million shards. He stared at the neckpiece still clenched in his fist, as though his hand belonged to someone else. Part of him was on the outside watching his actions with a weird sense of detachment.

Sacha had flinched back, and the sight momentarily stunned him. Had he really just roared those words at her? Smashed her bottle of wine like some wife-beating bastard? But the ferocity within him blazed over to remind him that *she* was the one who'd brought them to this point.

"That uncontrollable rage you're feeling, it's only going to get worse." Her quiet words grated against his simmering anger. "I can help you learn to control it, but that outburst just highlights why I'm doing this. You need stability and permanence. Volatile emotion is not your friend at the moment. Trying to make a relationship out of that will only end in disaster, and I care about you too much to let that happen."

Through the haze of receding ire and rising emotional exhaustion, her words made sense, but that didn't make them any easier to process. He looked at Sacha, but only saw pain. His body clenched, and the vague sense of nausea returned. He couldn't do pain; he'd had enough of that this past year and a half.

"I can't be here right now." His words came out rough as he turned away from her, and he swallowed over his tight throat. "I'm sorry about the mess."

"Kai—"

He skirted the kitchen bench, striding through the apartment as fast as he could without actually running. Running wouldn't help, because all of the things he wanted to escape were stuck inside of him.

Chapter Thirteen

Kai lifted a heavy hand and used his forearm to wipe at the sweat dripping down his face. The silence pressed in on him, but he shut the thought down because it wasn't really that quiet. If he listened hard enough, he could hear the slight vibrating hum of the ship's various electronics, the slight whoosh of the air system, voices echoing from somewhere nearby, and a whole lot of other white noise he couldn't identify.

Life was happening, the same as it did every day and night on board the *Valiant Knox*, and he was just sitting, feeling the burn in his muscles and cooling sweat over his skin.

A blissful numbness had set in a while ago, about the same time as he'd lost count on how many reps he'd done at the weight machine. Luckily, at this time of night, the officers' gym was empty, so there hadn't been anyone around to see him pumping weights heavier than he should be attempting less than a week out of prison camp, forcing himself through each blazing, aching repetition like a man possessed. No, not *like* a man possessed, he was a man possessed; demons of captivity riding his soul like a damned carnival sideshow.

At least the punishing weight set had resulted in exactly what he'd wanted—exhausting his body to the point his mind could no longer function, bringing with it that all-encompassing lack of sensation he had going on. It had worn away the last of his anger, stopped Sacha's words from circling around and around in his mind, and then finally given him respite from the vague panicky feeling he'd been trying to ignore all day.

With slow, heavy movements, he dragged the towel from where he'd draped it across the padded bench seat earlier, and then swiped it over his face and neck. Maybe now he could face the fact that since he had nowhere else to stay, he had to take himself back to Sacha's apartment, like a damn whipping boy who didn't know any better. Though the bank had found his money, they hadn't finished setting up his new account and returning the funds. Maybe he needed to follow up with them in the morning.

"Lifting without a spotter? You're looking for trouble."

Alpha had come into the gym and stopped in front of him. Kai had been so lost in his thoughts, he hadn't even noticed. He mopped the towel over the back of his neck, and then left the cloth draped across his shoulders. "What are you doing here at this time of night?"

With a shrug, Alpha moved to sit on a nearby bench. "Sacha messaged me. She was worried about you, but she didn't think you'd want to see her."

Ah, hell. Guilt and shame spiraled through him in a stinging burn, blackening his insides. "What happened, it wasn't—"

"She didn't tell me anything." Alpha held up his hands in a gesture to stop him. "And you certainly don't need to tell me. She just wanted to know if I'd seen you. I didn't tell her I was looking for you. And if you hadn't been here, I probably would've given up pretty quickly."

Kai breathed a sigh of relief. The last thing he wanted was to talk about what had happened in Sacha's kitchen, not when he'd been doing his damnedest in the last few hours to forget.

"How's your injured pilot. Orman, was it?"

Alpha's expression sobered. "Alive. That's about the best I can say. He suffered critical oxygen deprivation, along with some minor burns and contusions. They say if he wakes up, he'll probably have some brain damage. He definitely won't ever fly a V-29 again. Another good man lost."

For a long moment they were both silent. He didn't know about Alpha, but all the men under his command who'd been lost were crowding his head. This war had been too long and costly. Decades worth of fighting and death.

As the shadows of the dead faded, his thoughts rolled back around to that CS Soldier. Would Alpha believe him? Though he might be willing to risk the reputation of his sanity to do the right thing, he wanted to be in a position where people would be less likely to question his memory.

Proof. He just needed proof, and then they wouldn't think twice about interrogating the man.

"Doesn't it seem like we're stuck in stasis?" Alpha muttered. "We're not winning this goddamn war, though we're certainly not losing it. All we're doing is holding lines. And I can't believe those bastards had you for over a year and never said a word about it."

"Probably because they knew if news got out they were holding a commander, the entire UEF would ride on up to Ilari and blow them off the face of the planet. We might be at war, but there are rules about that sort of thing." He massaged just above his bad knee, a small echo of pain throbbing through his bones. Those bastards had spent the first half of his confinement trying to get whatever information they could out of him and Amos. They'd been especially interested in the upper-workings of the UEF, questioning him about the people in charge and UEF protocol. He'd told them as little as possible. And when they'd gotten sick of that game, they'd spent the second half trying to *convert* him to their belief that technology was the basis of all modern sin and greed. "I'm sure the brass will want to hold that card close to their chest so they can bring it out at a time when it'll cause the CSS maximum damage."

"You know Cam has gone to Defcon One in the past few days? He's been trying to convince Emmanuel that we need to call in extra forces and retaliate hard for what they did to you."

"Is that why he came up here? I just assumed it was the usual briefing about current ground deployments." He shook his head, clenching his fist around the damp towel.

The ones directly responsible for his imprisonment deserved whatever the UEF could bring down on them, but that left 90 percent of Ilari's population who didn't have anything to do with it. "It won't change anything, and you know the ones who suffer most are the civilians."

"Damn true." Alpha crossed his arms and shifted on the bench. "I'm not going to ask how you've been doing since you got back. You're probably sick of people asking. But I assume you didn't get the five-star accommodations at the CSS Enlightening Camp."

Kai's lips twisted into a grim smile, though even that expression felt false. "I sure as hell didn't. I'm doing about as well as you'd think. The psyche would probably tell you I'm a textbook case for PTSD. Sacha seems to think so."

"Uh-huh." The non-verbal word sounded heavy with unspoken questions. "Well, I can tell you Sacha seems better since you got back. A bit brighter, more like her old self."

A warm torrent of relief cut right through the middle of the cold, dark feelings he'd been fighting since leaving Sacha's apartment. Selfishly, he hadn't given much thought as to whether she was worse or better off for his return, but he was glad to hear she seemed to be doing better. His instincts had been right in sensing they needed each other to recover from their separate traumas.

"Sacha will always be Sacha; she's too damn practical for her own good." He dragged a hand across the lower half of his face.

"Yeah, I bet she's giving you the doctor treatment twenty-four-seven."

"You have no idea." She'd let her doctor mask slip for a short time last night, and it had been everything he needed, everything they both needed. But since his meltdown she seemed to be hiding behind it more securely than ever. How was he supposed to get through to her as a friend, or something more?

"She probably wants you to talk it all out, but you know whenever you need to hang and *not* talk, I'm around. I can't even begin to imagine where your head is at right now."

"Believe me, you're better off not knowing," he muttered. "I don't even want to face what this has done to me, so I don't know how anyone else would. It's ugly, Leigh. And everyone can sit here imagining what I went through, but it probably still wouldn't be half as bad as the reality."

Alpha leaned forward and gripped his shoulder. "PTSD is nothing to be ashamed of. We all know guys who've had it and come out fine on the other side. Frankly, if you *weren't* showing signs of it, I'd be worried. I've seen some pretty horrible crap out there on the frontlines myself, and some nights it's all I can do to sweat out the darkness and wait for morning."

He stared at his friend, and caught the shadows in Alpha's eyes, the same ones he saw in himself whenever he looked in the mirror.

"Thanks, brother." Kai shifted closer to return his friend's grip for a long moment. "I know I'm not the first soldier, or the only soldier, to go through this, but in that moment—"

"When there's nothing but the panic, it's hard to remember." Alpha sent him a grim smile, before standing. "I've got to get up to squadron level, but we'll catch up for a drink when I'm off-shift tomorrow."

"Sure thing." He waved as Alpha walked out of the gym again, leaving him in solitary contemplation.

Scenes from earlier in the night went on live-action-replay in his head. And with each moment, shame wormed through his guts, because he didn't recognize the guy who'd all but fallen apart in Sacha's kitchen. Was this his life now? A sense of jagged disconnection had struck deep in his soul and cemented into place, the old Kai unable to assimilate with the new Kai.

Maybe she had been right about them, but not for the reasons she'd given. Maybe she'd had second thoughts when she'd woken up in the morning and thought about Elliot. Maybe she felt like she'd betrayed his memory or something, and was using her role as his doctor as an excuse to distance herself.

He couldn't really blame her. How could he ever be the man she needed him to be, when apparently he couldn't even cook a meal without having a panic attack, or navigate a thorny conversation without blowing a gasket and smashing up her kitchen? He didn't want to be that guy, and Sacha definitely didn't deserve that kind of man in her life.

Yet a quiet sense of desperation for her had pierced his heart, and wouldn't be dislodged. She might not need him, but he sure as hell needed her, even if she wasn't willing to give all of what he wanted. The idea of going back to sleep at her apartment tonight soothed as much as pained him.

He rubbed the middle of his chest and stood with a long exhale. His life was a mess, like someone had set it on top of a landmine and stepped back to watch it splatter. He couldn't ever put the pieces back to how they used to be, and maybe part of him had been trying to do that with her last night. All he could do was scrape up the usable bits he could find and work out a new way to mush it all together. As for how long that would take, well, trying to work that out would likely send him into another meltdown.

Instead, he concentrated on the now. Putting away the damp towel and taking himself back down to her apartment. And damned if he wasn't a coward for hoping she'd be asleep.

Chapter Fourteen

Sacha checked the readout on the screen monitoring the fighter pilot's brain activity. He was comatose, but the occasional heightened activity gave her hope he might wake up. However, the spikes were happening less and less often, which wasn't a good sign. He seemed to be slipping away, and frustration swirled low through her, because there wasn't a damn thing she could do about it.

She walked out of the room, releasing a low sigh. Her frustration wasn't solely directed toward the unfortunate situation with the fighter pilot.

After the blowout in her kitchen last night, Kai hadn't come home by the time she'd gone to bed. In all the years she'd known him, she'd never seen him display that kind of rage before. And while calm logic told her it all came back to the PTSD and his time as a POW, it didn't help settle the roiling emotions within her. Didn't help lessen the worry she'd stewed in while she'd waited for him to return and resisted the urge to go out searching the ship for him. At least he'd been there, asleep on the couch, when she'd left this morning. She didn't know what she would have done if he'd failed to come home at all.

Worst of all, she couldn't help blaming herself. Was it a coincidence that the first real cracks in his mental state had shown after they'd been together? Had the emotional intimacies between them deeply affected him in a negative way, just as she'd feared?

She couldn't talk to anyone about this, because if they knew what had happened, not only would she be removed from his case, and possibly forbidden from seeing him, but she could face disciplinary charges for unprofessional conduct.

Yet selfishly, part of her didn't regret what had happened between them. It had eased places inside her that had been hurting too long. If not for everything standing between them, she would have thrown herself into a relationship with Kai wholeheartedly. Instead, she had probably destroyed the potential of anything good ever being between them by giving in to her own self-centered desires and taking things to the one place she'd known they shouldn't go.

Her med-comm vibrated, and she muttered a short *thank god* for the distraction. However, just as she wrapped her fingers around it, a siren started up, echoing throughout the ship. The sirens didn't sound on the *Knox* very often; it had only happened one other time in all the years she'd been serving onboard the ship. Even as she snapped the comm off her belt, she could already guess what she'd see.

Code Alpha-One, Commerce Level. All available medico personnel to mobilize.

Adrenaline surging, she shoved the med-comm back onto her belt and ran for the nearest storeroom to grab an emergency pack. Other nurses and sub-doctors were already there, working in controlled chaos to prepare the med-level for mass casualties. Alpha-One was a critical code, meaning either the ship was under attack, or there'd been a major incident onboard with death confirmed. Considering the call was to commerce level, she doubted they were under attack, which meant something bad had happened in the trade sector of the ship.

They'd all practiced drills for this kind of thing, and each person knew their role, whether it was to stay on med-level and take in the wounded, or be one of the first responders on scene of the incident. As she hurried through med-level to get up to commerce, it seemed like everyone was falling back on their training just as they should be, which made her job that much easier.

She joined the group of first responders and hurried into the levels above. As they stepped out of the transit-porter, the acidic taste of smoke hit the back of her throat, and she passed groups of people evacuating. There were a couple of military guards standing nearby, coordinating people getting on and off the transits. She snagged the attention of the nearest one.

"Hey! Where are we needed?"

"Port side, food sector, ma'am."

She called a thanks over her shoulder as she led her group into the thickening smoke. She could hear the loud *vroom* of the environmentals above them, working to take the deadly fumes out of the air. She reached into the side of her pack and yanked out a small, light oxygen breather, snapping it over her face and then glancing back to make sure her people were doing the same.

As they reached the sector where most of the restaurants, cafés, and other eateries were, she could see flames burning out from beneath the awnings of a take-away. Military guys manned hoses, spraying a gray fire-dousing foam over the front of the shop. Bloodied and burned people lay and sat in the thoroughfare a little way down from the destroyed shop, but not far enough from possible danger.

"Let's get a temporary triage set up near the transit-porters and start moving these people. Make sure everyone has a mask, especially those fighting the fire," she said to the first responders. She took a quick moment to comm Macaulay and organized a second group of responders to help deal with this faster.

As she snapped on a pair of gloves, she caught sight of a too-familiar form in amongst the uniformed military people managing the hoses. She grabbed another mask from her pack and hurried forward, feeling the heat from the fire baking over her as she got closer.

Kai saw her, and handed his spot on the hose off to another soldier nearby. He jogged over, coughing under where he had his T-shirt pulled up over his face. He was streaked in soot and blood, his eyes red and watering. She reached up and helped him get into the mask, before grabbing his elbow and pulling him farther away from the raging fire.

"Kai, what are you doing here?"

For a moment he didn't answer her, gulping air in the mask. She tightened her hold on him. Had he been near the fast-food place when it caught fire? Had she almost lost him again? The thought ripped through her, leaving her knees weak for a dizzying second.

"I was at the BUE branch, signing off on my new accounts, when I heard the explosion."

"Explosion?" That was worse than a simple fire. There would be more casualties, with more extensive injuries.

He nodded, taking a few more deep breaths. "I came down here and started getting people out before the fire took hold."

She glared at him. "You should have waited for the first responders. What if there'd been a second explosion?"

"Then there'd be more people dead. I couldn't stand by and watch those injured people burn."

She reached up and wrapped her other hand over his shoulder. "You don't always have to be the hero. That's what got Elliot killed."

His gaze softened as he stared down at her. "I'm okay, Sacha."

She pulled back from him, the cold fear of what could have happened to him, what had happened to her husband, leaving chills beneath her skin.

"Elliot used to tell me the same thing, until he wasn't okay anymore." For the first time in months, those awful feelings she'd struggled through after losing Kai and then Elliot were too close to the surface. But she couldn't deal with that in this second, she had a job to do; people were relying on her. "I have patients I need to see."

She started to turn away, but Kai grabbed her hand.

"Wait, Sacha. There's something else."

She glanced back at him, too on edge to talk when her emotions had just been scraped raw, and there were casualties needing her help.

"Kai, I need to go—"

"No, it's important. This is it. This is the place where I lost that soldier."

She shook her head, not comprehending his meaning. "What are you saying?"

He stepped closer to her, a determined, almost fanatical gleam in his gaze. "I told you, remember? That soldier I followed, he was acting suspicious. He stopped outside this burger joint, and then I lost him. I don't think this is a coincidence. I don't think this was an accident."

A defeated kind of emotional weariness slipped through her. Kai was getting worse, and she couldn't do anything about it right this second, not when so many critically injured people were waiting to be treated.

"Kai, can you hear yourself? You know it sounds paranoid, right? Do you really think the CSS are sophisticated or organized enough to infiltrate the *Valiant Knox* as one of our own? And why blow up a burger shop?"

His expression took on an edge of frustrated anger. "You don't even want to consider for one second that I might be right, do you? All you can do is look at me through your doctor's lenses and tell me I'm going nuts. I don't know why—"

He broke off and looked up, dawning comprehension in his gaze. "No, I think I do know why. And I'm going to prove it."

He yanked out his comm and she shook her head. A second wave of medico responders had turned up, and they'd started moving people down to the triage. She needed to get Kai off this level and squared away somewhere safe until this crisis had been dealt with.

She looked back at him, to see he was talking on his comms with someone. The conversation was short, and he had a grim look of satisfaction to him as he put his comm away again.

"Do you know what's above us?"

"No, but how about you tell me while I take you home so you can get cleaned up?"

"Don't patronize me." He pointed a finger outward. "All of the port-side launch decks are above us. The fire has gone into the outer hull, and Alpha just confirmed it's interfering with the hatchways. As of this moment, more than three-quarters of the *Knox*'s launch bays are useless."

A jolt of shock rammed into her. If the ship was attacked or something happened on Ilari, the *Knox* wouldn't be able to provide adequate air reinforcements. Had Kai been right after all?

But this wasn't her problem. She was a doctor, and she was needed at the emergency triage.

"Kai, I can't think about this right now. Maybe you do have a point, but I think it would be better if you went home, had a shower—"

"I am not leaving in the middle of a crisis." His voice came out low and furious, reminiscent of the old Commander Yang who'd sent soldiers scurrying with a single look. "You might not believe me, you might think I'm damaged or fragile, but I'm not going to sit on this any longer. I don't care if it's risking my return to duty. I have an obligation to protect everyone onboard the *Knox*, even if they're not under my command any longer. I'm going to Emmanuel with this, which is what I should have done days ago." He stared past her, and for a split second, the yellow-orange of the flames reflected in his eyes. "Maybe I could have stopped this, if I'd come forward sooner."

Before she could reply, he turned and stalked away from her, his posture tight and shoulders back. Instead of making him crumble, this horrible situation seemed to have strengthened his fortitude.

She turned to look at the lowering flames and last few casualties being moved from the thoroughfare. Was this tragedy partly her fault? Yet, she'd been so sure he was just displaying PTSD symptoms. For the first time, the notion that she may have been wrong, *so very wrong*, dug deep, burning claws into her.

• • •

A gentle hand gripped her shoulder, her name murmured quietly, waking her from the doze she'd fallen into. She blinked open her eyes to see Kai standing above her. He wore nothing but a pair of sweats. His hair was wet and he smelled clean and soapy, as though he'd just come out of the shower. She pushed herself straighter, glancing at the clock on the kitchen wall that read after one a.m.

"Sorry, Sacha, but you're currently occupying my bed."

"Oh, sorry." She brushed off the blanket that had been covering her legs and sat up, touching her feet to the floor. "What happened when you went to see Emmanuel?"

She'd tried calling him a few times after the initial rush of injured patients had passed, but he hadn't answered, and hadn't returned any of her calls.

He sat on the arm of the chair adjacent to the couch and dropped his attention away from her, avoiding her gaze.

"You were partly right. At first Emmanuel was skeptical about my memory, too. But we talked things out, and when we brought in Cam, he confirmed that my suspicions put some pieces together that hadn't made sense to him before. He'd already thought there was something not right about the soldier. We made some discreet enquiries. It seems he might have killed a UEF soldier and taken the man's place. The only thing worse is that he may have had help from the inside, because someone altered the bio-ID on the dead soldier's file to match the imposter. There's a possibility the infiltration already runs deep."

Her heart thudded hard against her ribs. Oh god, Kai had been right, and she'd been trying to convince him it was all in his head. Her throat tightened and she tried to swallow down the aching tension.

"What's going to happen now?"

He shrugged one shoulder. "If we can find the bastard, he'll be apprehended and questioned. Unfortunately, a search of the ship turned up nothing, so he either managed to stow away on a shuttle headed for the ground while we were all distracted, or he's hiding somewhere, which isn't impossible on a ship this size. Either way, he's our number one priority. We need to know if there are any other moles in our ranks, and what else the CSS is planning."

She nodded, though he wasn't looking at her. Not that she blamed him. She'd been so focused on treating him as a patient she'd become a terrible friend.

But hadn't she already had the same conversation with herself, about not knowing how to be his friend? And it seemed she hadn't been a very good doctor for him, either. A sense of failure pressed in on her from all sides.

"I'm sorry, Kai." The words came out as a broken whisper. He still didn't look at her, though a muscle clenched in his jaw.

"It doesn't matter now, what's done is done."

Empty words, with no real meaning behind them. Was this really what she'd brought them to?

She wanted to reach out to him, make physical contact because she knew in that, at least, they had been in the same place for a time, connected in a way they never had before. But she'd gone and destroyed that as well. The tension in him, his closed-off posture and tight expression, told her he wouldn't welcome anything from her in that moment. Considering the position she'd put him in, she didn't deserve any less.

She pushed up from the couch and brushed by him, heading for her room without saying a word. He didn't try to stop her, didn't say a single thing to call her back or clear the air between them. If he felt anything like she did, then she supposed he realized there was nothing left to say.

Chapter Fifteen

Sacha took her oversized mug out of the coffeemaker and then blew at the steam swirling off the top, ignoring the clock on the wall that would no doubt tell her she'd worked through dinner again. Her grumbling stomach was already giving her enough grief over it. She'd grab something to eat on the way home in a little while, but she had another handful of reports she wanted to get through.

Besides, the longer she stayed away from her apartment, the less time she'd spend alternately criticizing and congratulating herself. Yes, she'd screwed up in not listening to Kai about recognizing that soldier, but if she'd been wanting to drive a wedge between them to prevent any more intimate moments, she couldn't have come up with a better way.

As she rounded the end of the passageway leading to her office, she spotted Macaulay coming out of his office across the way, the light on the panel in the bulkhead flashing red into lock mode as he stepped away from the door.

"Dalton, why are you still here?" He shot her a frown as he stopped, though his expression was mostly exasperated. "This is the third night in a row you've been here for hours on end."

A bristling indignation simmered up within her. "I'm busy. You're busy. We're all really busy since the explosion on commerce level, so excuse me if I want to catch up on a few things."

He shifted closer, his expression softening into something too close to pity. "I don't blame you for throwing yourself into your work for a distraction. But you need to start bringing it back a notch, otherwise you're going to burn yourself out. Today is almost over, you got through it, and it'll get easier every year."

She stared at him, her brain trying to catch up, because apparently she'd missed half the conversation. "Today?"

"You know, your—"

Even as he started saying the words, the answer burst into her mind like a bubble that had been slowly expanding in the background, releasing a whitewash of guilt and remorse through her body.

"My wedding anniversary," she whispered over a thick tongue. The first since Elliot had died, the inaugural one marking her as a widow.

Oh god. How could she have forgotten? Well, actually, she hadn't entirely forgotten. Last week, before Kai had turned up, the thought of getting closer to this day had consumed her every waking moment. She hadn't known how she'd get through the day without breaking down, how she'd endure all the sympathetic well-wishers, or what she was supposed to do with herself

Except, ever since she'd walked into that med-bay and seen Kai lying on the gurney, she hadn't given her upcoming wedding anniversary a single thought. Now the day had come, and she *still* hadn't remembered, not until Macaulay had reminded her. In fact, the day was nearly over, and she hadn't devoted one moment of remembrance to her dead husband.

The guilt tripled, closing around her chest and squeezing until air was hard to find. "I'm sorry, Macaulay, I've been a mess these past few days. You know, I think I will head home."

She spun away from him before he could reply, because her heart was beating too hard and her eyes were beginning to sting. But she couldn't break down yet, not until she'd reached her apartment, where she could be alone to berate herself over this betrayal to Elliot. It wasn't enough that she'd broken her oath as a doctor and slept with Kai, possibly hindering his recovery, and then failed to believe him about the CS Soldier, but to forget the most important day of her life with Elliot?

God, I'm a horrible person.

The escape down to the residential levels of the ship went by in a blur, until she got inside her apartment and sank down on the couch. She gulped in a hard breath, but she'd held off falling apart for so long, it seemed like her body couldn't let go. The grief was trapped inside her, thrashing around like a wild animal. She wanted to let it out, needed to force it free, but she'd wound herself up so tight, she could only sit there, her body aching with tension and crushing emotions.

"Sacha?"

She squeezed her eyes closed at Kai's voice behind her. Though he'd come back to sleep on the couch the last three nights, they hadn't really seen each other, with her working late and him out doing who-knew-what. And they certainly hadn't talked to each other.

She couldn't face him, not when the truth of her selfish perfidy had been stripped bare. Why did he have to be here just in time to catch her in one of the darkest moments of her life?

She stood on unsteady legs. A few steps to her room, and she could endure her shame spiral in private.

She'd made it halfway across the room, her gaze focused on the doorway to her bedroom, but Kai caught her wrist.

"Sacha, what's happened?" He tugged her arm gently, urging her to turn around, but she kept her face averted. "Is this about the other night? I'm sorry, I know you probably think I'm angry with you, but the truth is I'm more furious with myself."

She stared at their feet on the soft carpet. "It's okay. I'm not upset about that."

"Has something else happened?" His fingers touched her chin. "Did you lose a patient or something?"

She shook her head free of his touch and stepped back, wrapping her arms around her middle. "I forgot. This is the one day I should have remembered, and I had totally forgotten until Macaulay mentioned it just now. Do you know how awful that is?"

"You forgot…?" Kai shifted closer to her again, and *damn him*, but she wanted to sink against his chest, bury her face, and maybe not feel so bad for half a second.

Instead, she turned away from him to stare at the picture

of her and Elliot she had displayed on a side table, along with a few of his special possessions, things that reminded her of good times.

"My wedding anniversary."

"Oh, Sacha." Kai's hands closed around her upper arms, but she shrugged out of his grip.

"Don't. I don't deserve it. What kind of person forgets their own wedding anniversary less than a year after they've buried their husband?" She blew out a shuddering breath, wanting to let go of the profound anguish within her, to simply let the grief drag her under, but terrified that once she did it would take days, weeks, maybe even months to resurface, just like it had after Elliot had been killed.

"Sacha, you are not a terrible person." He grabbed hold of her again, this time keeping a firm grip on her.

"Let me go, I need to be alone right now." She squirmed harder, but he spun her to face him, before wrapping his arms around her.

"No. Locking yourself in your room and crucifying yourself over this won't make it any better, and it certainly won't change things." He cupped her face and urged her to look up at him.

Her control slipped a notch, leaving the thinnest thread holding her together. She didn't have the strength to fight him.

"You've put so much effort into me since I got back. Elliot wouldn't be upset with you over forgetting. He'd want us looking out for each other." His fingers eased into her hair in a soothing caress, but the action only put her more on edge. "I don't think it's surprising, or a sin, that you forgot about today. But don't disrespect Elliot's memory by punishing yourself over a small mistake. He wouldn't want that."

Kai talking so casually about this, as if it wasn't such a big deal, was the pressure that ended up snapping everything inside of her. She jerked back out of his hold, a tidal wave of dark emotions burning and blackening everything in its path as it surged through her.

"Don't tell me what Elliot would have wanted! You might have been his friend, but I was his *wife*." She spun and snatched up the picture of her and Elliot from the side table with shaking hands. "And what did I do before he'd even been gone a year? I screwed his best friend and forgot our wedding anniversary all in the same week."

A short hysterical laugh escaped, even as a few tears streaked down her face. It was almost funny, exactly how far she'd messed up everything in her life.

"Sacha—" Kai held up his hands in a placating gesture.

"No!" She pointed a trembling finger at him. "Don't stand there and try to tell me it's all okay. It's not okay!"

She threw the picture, but Kai stooped down to catch it before it hit the floor and shattered. *Damn him*. She stepped forward and shoved him in both shoulders as he straightened.

"Why couldn't you just let it smash? I failed him, and I failed you. I don't want to have to look at him and be reminded of every messed up thing about my life."

Kai set the picture down and then stepped toward her. "Sacha, this is just the grief talking—"

"Now who is being patronizing?" More tears flowed down her face, but she didn't care anymore. "Don't talk to me about grief. You have no idea how deep that scar runs."

He rubbed the back of his neck, concern and frustration

in his expression as he stared at her. She could tell he wanted to say something else, to help her in some way. But there was nothing he could do. She was alone in this, just like she'd been since the day Elliot had died. A dark ferocity came on the heels of her sorrow, and she couldn't stand him looking at her like that a moment longer, as if she were broken, as if she wasn't the same person any longer. It might be true, but she didn't want to face the reality of that in his infuriatingly sympathetic gaze.

She turned away from him, but came face to face with the little shrine of mementos she'd set up for Elliot, now missing the picture of him. She clamped her hands on the edge of the table, barely restraining the urge to swipe the surface clean, like she wished she could do to her own conscience.

"Just leave me alone, Kai. I don't want anything from you."

She heard him shuffle a step closer. "I don't think you should be alone—"

"Get out!" She shoved herself away from the table and escaped into her room, not waiting to see if Kai had complied with her shouted order. Part of her expected him to start banging and demanding she let him in like he had the first night he'd stayed here. But as she laid herself on top of the coverlet with slow, stiff movements, nothing but silence came to her.

Chapter Sixteen

Kai flicked his hand, signaling the barkeep, and watched as Harley Gregson poured the third double shot for the night.

"What's the legendary Commander Yang doing in a place like this, drinking alone at this time of night?" Harley set the bottle to the side and then leaned his forearms against the bar.

"What's the owner of this bar doing pouring shots? Don't you have employees to do that for you?" Kai saluted with his glass and then knocked back the liquor. He'd known the owner of Harley's Bar for almost as many years as he'd been onboard the *Valiant Knox*. Harley's was the place all the military staff came to hang out when they were off-shift, and at some point over the years, he'd become friends with the guy who ran the establishment.

Harley sent him a half smile. "You know as well as I do, if you want to keep the riffraff under control, you've got to put in an appearance and randomly order people around every now and then."

"Spoken like a true commander. Want to switch jobs?"

The barkeep straightened with a grimace. "No way. There was a reason I went into private commerce instead of joining the UEF. You can keep your laced-up boots and regulations coming out the wazoo, thank you very much."

Kai shrugged one shoulder and motioned to his glass again. "Suit yourself."

Harley poured him another double shot. "Sorry, Commander, but after this I'm cutting you off. Can't have you getting plastered in my fine establishment."

"I think I'm still half a dozen drinks away from getting plastered. And where else am I supposed to drink myself into oblivion?" He sent Harley a glare as he sipped at the drink.

"I believe the point is that Commander Yang shouldn't be getting wasted at all. Aren't there rules about that sort of thing?"

He grinned, starting to feel the buzz from the alcohol. "Ah, but you see, I'm technically not a commander anymore. No one knows what I am. Emmanuel gave me administrative duties until they can work out what to do with me, which makes me his office bitch. And last I checked, the commander's office bitch can get smashed off his face whenever he feels like it."

"Oh yeah? Well I'll need to see that ridiculous demotion in writing. Until then, no commanders getting drunk in my bar." Harley shot him a smart-ass grin, before sauntering away to put the bottle back on the shelf.

Kai took another sip of his drink, trying to make it last. He'd never been much of a drinker anyway, could count on one hand the number of times he'd gotten really drunk, and that had been when he was young and stupid. There were rules about senior officers overindulging, even when they weren't on-shift. Yet after the week he'd had—the last three days in particular spent unsuccessfully searching for the soldier suspected in the bombing—topped off by the blow-out with Sacha earlier, surely he could be forgiven for indulging in a few too many drinks.

He rubbed the middle of his chest, that now-familiar ache returning. *Ah, hell.* That usually preceded some kind of *moment*, whether it be a deluge of bad memories he didn't want to face, or a few long moments where he couldn't find enough air to breathe... And most frustrating, he couldn't work out what set him off. The psychologist had said they would work through it, but everything would take time, there was no magic overnight cure.

He didn't want to take time, he wanted to be over it so he could get on with his life. Except, that in itself was a problem, because he had no damn clue what shape his life would take from here on out. At least Emmanuel had gotten him back onto the UEF payroll, so he could afford things like the fine whiskey he'd been indulging in for the past hour.

To be fair, he probably should've used some of that money to get some new accommodations, but he just couldn't bring himself to leave Sacha. Her emotional state when she'd come home this evening worried him and, on top of everything else going on, he couldn't handle the idea of being totally cut off from her.

Although, after what had happened tonight, maybe that was a good thing. It had broken his heart seeing her all but falling apart, the grief over Elliot she'd apparently been hiding forcing itself free. After she'd rebuffed his comfort and locked herself in her room, he'd sat numbly on her couch, wishing he could do something, *anything,* to make her pain go away. By the time he'd come to terms with the fact that she wouldn't let him be her safe harbor, and things between them really were that broken, his insides had felt scraped raw.

Ever since he'd returned to the *Knox,* he and Sacha had caused each other pain. He'd thought after what his time in prison had done to both of them, they'd become closer, lean on each other equally to get through the hard times and dark, lonely nights. Instead, they were only tearing further apart.

So, just this damned once, he'd wanted to have a few too many drinks and maybe not feel so bad about everything for five minutes. But even as he finished his last shot, the warm, fuzzy glow was fleeting, and dark things started stirring in the deepest corners of his mind where he refused to shine a light. That constricted feeling in his chest got tighter, pumping up his heart rate to crash against the inside of his ribs.

"No, no, no," he muttered, dragging a hand down his face, as if that could wipe his mind clean. The flashes started, like last time in Sacha's kitchen, jagged pictures with no sense or reference, just horrific images flaring one after another.

"So, is this what you've been doing with yourself for the past three nights when you've stayed out so late?"

Kai glanced over his shoulder, the sound of Sacha's voice momentarily shoving back the reel of horror. He hadn't expected to see her again tonight, not after the mini-meltdown she'd had.

She stood two steps behind him, her arms crossed and

an extremely unimpressed frown on her face. Her hair fell free, but tousled around her shoulders, and she'd changed out of her work uniform into a casual loose shirt and simple pair of curve-hugging jeans, as if the scene in her apartment hadn't happened.

"Kai, you know it's not a good idea for someone with PTSD to drink excessively, it can lead to substance abuse—"

Her words faded in and out, as though someone was playing with the volume control, and the flashes flickered back to life, stronger and clearer this time, bringing a cold, clammy sense of suffocation with them.

"I need to get out of here," he mumbled, sliding off the barstool unsteadily.

"How many have you had?" She reached for him, but he dodged her grip.

He shook his head and turned away from her, blindly bumping into someone else as the images roared higher through his mind… Screams from the other prisoners echoing eerily off the concrete walls like souls trapped in hell. Robed figures leaning over him, holding burning crucifixes against his skin, Amos, drenched in blood from a head wound that had taken too long to heal, the sound of fighter jets overhead, so close, yet too far away to help them, the three minutes of sunshine they saw every day, and Amos's complexion, waxy-gray from death.

He stumbled out of the bar and then stopped to lean heavily against a nearby bulkhead, chest heaving, because he couldn't get enough damned air again, and he could smell the dungeon—death, desperation, and sour cold. He shuddered, swallowing convulsively at the whiskey burning up the back of his throat.

"Kai, here, I got you some water." Sacha pressed something cool into his hand, and he rode out a clammy shiver before straightening far enough to gulp the contents in the glass.

The water washed the sick feeling back down, and at last the gruesome replay subsided, leaving him with that dull, damaged sensation he wished he could cleanse himself of.

"This isn't the answer, Kai."

Neck muscles aching, he lifted his heavy head and focused on her.

"Seriously, I know what you're going through is hard, but becoming an alcoholic—"

His fist contracted around the empty glass. "So that's what you think of me now? That I could actually use liquor to escape my problems? When have you ever known me to take the easy way out?"

She crossed her arms and turned away for a moment, her expression tightening before she looked back at him. "The old Kai would never have resorted to this. He would have faced his problems head on. But you're a different person now, we both are. There's no use trying to live our lives by the way we used to be."

"You really think I've changed that much?"

"Haven't you?" She motioned to him. "Just look at how I found you tonight."

The uncontrollable fury that had taken over him a few nights ago in her kitchen stirred, so he bent to set the glass on the floor between his boots and the bulkhead. This time, he would not let the rage control him.

"I'm not drunk. That was another one of those panic attacks I'm *not* having. Since you're a doctor, I would've thought you could tell the difference. And I don't know what you expect. I'm seeing the psychologist, I'm fully aware I have PTSD, but I'm dealing, and I'm still in control. *You're* the one who won't admit how things really are. You want me to work through the things that have caused me pain, yet what happened tonight tells me you haven't let yourself really deal with losing your husband. I thought we had something important, but all you seem capable of doing is pushing me away, using your job as a Band-Aid for the guilt you feel over Elliot."

As soon as the words left his mouth, he wanted to suck them back in again. But it couldn't be done, and the flash of hurt that crossed Sacha's face revived the guilt he'd been trying to outrun earlier tonight.

God, what had happened to them? How had they ended up *here*? Sacha had literally been his lifeline, his salvation when he'd been in that prison, thoughts of her keeping him strong and determined to get home. Yet now they had nothing but guilt and hurt between them. Did she really think him so weak that he would drown his problems in a bottle or three of liquor?

Sacha pushed back a thick lock of hair and sighed. "I don't know what to think. All I know is you've come home well after midnight the past three nights, and I just found you in Harley's. What else am I supposed to believe?"

And of course she'd avoided mentioning anything about herself or her own demons. A small swell of frustration swept through him.

"Well, you could start by not jumping to the worst conclusion. Ask Harley. This is the first night I've come up here. The other three nights I spent in the officers' gym. In case you haven't noticed, I've got some muscle mass to regain, and exercising myself into oblivion helps me sleep better."

A shadow of sympathy darkened her eyes, and he had to turn away from her before he completed the humiliation of the night by getting on his knees in front of her to beg. Not that he really had any clue what he'd be begging for, just that he was drowning in the need to have her make it all better for him.

Been there, done that, didn't turn out so well.

"I'm sorry, you're right, I shouldn't have jumped to conclusions. It's just been a long day."

He shrugged. "So let's call it a night."

She agreed and they started making their way toward the far end of the commerce level where the transit-porters were situated.

"Why did you come up here anyway? I thought you'd gone to bed for the night." He grimaced at the dull spasm of pain through his bad knee and altered his steps.

"When I woke up and found you gone, I guess I was a little worried about what you've been doing with yourself these past nights. And then I felt bad because I realized that I had kind of abandoned you, throwing myself into work so I didn't have to think about…well, everything."

"You take too much on yourself, Sacha. I'm not your responsibility. You're doing more than enough overseeing my medical care and sharing your home."

And it was true, even if it didn't feel like enough because he wanted more. It had long passed the time when he needed to face up to that.

"I think it's probably time I found my own place." Saying the words hurt, but he couldn't keep leeching off her just because the idea of being apart from her stole all higher reasoning from his brain. Which actually made no sense. He'd been on his own for a long time, had maintained a certain independence, even in the midst of the few relationships he'd had over the years. He'd never needed anyone else to help him work things out before, so why should now be any different?

Besides, she'd made her position clear where the two of them were concerned, and somehow since then, they'd almost become strangers to each other. Of all the things his time in the CSS Enlightening Camp had taken from him, this had to be the worst.

"Yes, I think you're right." Her words were careful, considered, as she slowed to a stop outside of a closed café. Her shoulders tightened into familiar determined lines as she faced him. "I should have been the one to suggest it, but I was also aware that you needed supervision — "

A sliver of grim humor threaded through him. "To make sure I didn't try to throw myself out the nearest hatch, or go on mind-numbing benders? I don't need a damned babysitter, Sacha. I've overseen more than a few POWs return to duty. I know the risks. I'll be fine on my own. You can check in on me whenever you want."

Her stance appeared to relax slightly. "Agreed. And for the record, I better not find you attempting any more binge drinking."

He stared back across the way to Harley's, his guts roiling uneasily. "No, I don't think I'll be doing that again."

If anything, the liquor had only weakened the tightly leashed control he'd been hanging on to in the past few days, and undone what little work he'd achieved in the few sessions he'd had with his psychologist.

Looked like he'd be back in the gym tomorrow night.

They continued walking toward the transit-porters in strained silence, and every step he took felt like he was walking away from her. But what else could he do? Despite what he felt for her, or maybe because of how he loved her, he should have moved from her apartment after he'd accidentally attacked her a few nights ago.

At the transit, they bid each other a short good night. Kai didn't let himself think too closely about things until he'd closed the door to the suite he'd rented at one of the *Knox*'s fancier hotels.

The quiet of the room pressed in on him as he sat on the edge of the bed and took in the opulent surroundings of the room specially reserved for visiting officers; easily three times the size of Sacha's modest apartment a few levels down.

He tiredly scrubbed a hand over his face, the not-so-fun effects of the liquor kicking in, starting with a pounding headache.

What the hell was he going to do?

Not just in terms of the situation with Sacha, but for the rest of his life. Did he really want to stay on the *Knox*, grasping at the existence he'd once had, with no way of ever returning things to how they'd once been? Was there really any shame in admitting he was a different soldier these days and taking the vice commodore position on Earth? It was one hell of a promotion, especially considering his age. Yet it would mean admitting the CSS had taken something from him the day they'd locked him up in that prison; the life he'd always expected to have.

However, going to Earth would take him away from the one bright thing in his life: Sacha. Except look at how that had turned out. Destroyed, like every other goddamn facet of his existence. They had a long history together, and he couldn't give up on that so easily, but he needed to do better for her, needed to know he wouldn't accidentally slash her throat in the kitchen.

Space and time. Despite how the notion shortened his breath and made his heart pound too hard, logically he knew they were the only things that could fix this situation. He needed to work through this on his own and prove he was worthy of her, to recover and reincarnate himself as a man she could trust with her safety and her heart. As vice commodore, he'd have all kinds of unlimited resources to achieve that, and more. His very soul ached at the idea of being so far away from her, but this was the best solution for her, for him. For them both.

Chapter Seventeen

Sacha pulled her surgical gown off, shoving the material into the laundry chute before heading into the scrub room. She rolled her shoulders, working out the tension after leaning over the table for the past few hours, repairing the vast internal damage her latest patient had suffered down on the frontlines.

Most of the straightforward medical procedures were handled on the ground at the hospital in the main UEF base, but serious cases were airlifted to the *Valiant Knox*, which had better equipment for the worst trauma cases; ones that would have been a death sentence a few hundred years ago.

Two relatively serene days had gone by since her wedding anniversary. That night, something inside of her had broken. Not in a bad way...it had actually been in a good way, like a noose releasing from around her neck.

Kai's words to her about Elliot had sunk deep into her psyche while she'd been sleeping, and she'd remembered the truth of who Elliot had been, and what he would have wanted for her.

Not only that, but the stark realization that she'd been a hypocrite had become crystal clear. She'd accused Kai of trying to focus on her to avoid dealing with the trauma of his captivity. After Elliot had died, she hadn't really dealt with his death, already struggling with the loss of Kai. Somehow, she had hit pause somewhere along the way and buried her feelings instead of working through them and moving on. Kai returning had been like ripping the bandages off a wound to find it had festered instead of healed.

That night he'd returned, too many feelings had ruptured through her, like a tidal surge from a broken pipe. But she hadn't allowed herself to dwell on them or even think about it too closely, instead she'd covered herself in her doctor's mantle and focused single-mindedly on Kai's issues.

She'd been doing exactly what she'd accused Kai of—using distractions to avoid dealing with the pain she'd pushed deep away inside her soul. The realization had been difficult, but significant.

The morning after their argument outside the bar, she'd gone off to her shift and had Macaulay take over the managing of Kai's ongoing medical care. Due to their conflicting shifts, and Kai still trying to track down the CS Soldier, they hadn't seen each other since. Probably not a bad thing until she could find the courage to admit how wrong she'd been.

She finished cleaning herself up, and then retrieved her datapad, reviewing her patient's information as she headed out of operating suits and through the ICU.

As she reached the doors that led to the offices, she was interrupted from reviewing the last part of a chart by a commotion from down the opposite hall. A shout echoed, followed by two male nurses running into one of the med-labs.

Sacha set her datapad into an empty data-slot in the bulkhead and hurried down the passageway, the shouting becoming more intense as she neared the med-lab.

She slammed through the door. "What's going—?"

Shock turned her feet to cement blocks as she took in the sight of two male nurses holding down Kai while a young female nurse attempted to give him some kind of shot.

He fought all three, thrashing hard enough that the female nurse couldn't get near him, while the two male nurses were almost lying on top of him, trying to hold him down. His gaze was wild, unseeing, and desperate, like the day they'd brought him home.

"Stop!" Her body suddenly remembered how to move and she leaped forward, but not fast enough. The female nurse had seen a small opening and ducked in to shove the dispenser against Kai's neck and pull the trigger, administering a shot of god-knew-what.

He roared and managed to throw off one of the male nurses, who crashed into a nearby trolley before going down.

"Give him a second dose," the other male nurse panted.

"No!" Sacha hip-and-shouldered her way in, knocking the young female nurse out of the way as she grabbed Kai's face. Beneath her fingers, his pulse was racing. "Kai, it's me. Calm down, okay? I'm right here with you."

He didn't seem to hear her, his body going slack as his struggling subsided.

"What did you give him?"

His pulse raced harder beneath his skin, and no one

answered her. She brought her head up, pinning the female nurse with a furious glare.

"What the hell did you give him?"

"J-just a sedative," the nurse stuttered. "He started having some kind of panic attack when I was taking his vitals. I followed procedure—"

"Did you read his chart before you started his vitals, or don't they teach you how to do that in med school any longer? Commander Yang is not meant to be given any kind of medication whatsoever, no matter the circumstances."

Sacha snatched a nearby sensor and then ripped Kai's shirt open, slapping the electrodes onto his chest. The screen above the bed flickered to life, bringing up his vitals. Even as the numbers registered, he went rigid, arching into a seizure.

"What's happening?" The female nurse shuffled back from the bed, her voice going up several notches.

"He's having a reaction to the sedative." Her voice came out sounding calm, and more than a little pissed off, not giving any hint to the absolute cold terror erupting from her soul.

They had no way of knowing what kind of drugs the CSS had been using on him while he'd been at the Enlightening Camp, and no clue how long they'd remain in his system. If she gave him anything to counteract the sedative, it might only make things worse. But then the decision got snatched out of her hands as Kai flatlined.

"I need ten cc's of a stimulant, let's go with drexaline." She spun to the trolley and grabbed another set of electrodes, these ones connected to the defibrillators.

Sacha got them connected up as someone pressed the dispenser gun into her palm. She took a second to swap out the hypodermic needle for a larger one, and then glanced at his face, his expression slack. Her heart stumbled in her chest, and for a second she forgot how to breathe. *Not the time to panic.* She swallowed down the rising dread.

"I'm sorry, Kai. This isn't going to be pretty."

She sucked in a sharp breath and then slammed the needle right into his heart. His body jerked as she shot the adrenaline into his system.

"Clear." She stepped back, and one of the male nurses hit the button to fire up the defibrillator.

The machine delivered a shock, jump-starting his heart on the first go. She let out a short breath, releasing some of the pent-up fear as she stepped forward again and removed the electrodes, replacing them with a handful of sensors.

The screen above the bed showed vitals settling into a normal range. Her mind went in to a slow spin, shock mixing with relief. On unsteady feet, she turned to stare at the three nurses.

"You will each write a detailed report about this incident, and submit it pending a review, before the end of shift tomorrow."

The female nurse started wringing her hands. "I'm sorry, I didn't think—"

"No, you didn't think. All of you are suspended for the rest of the day. And you can find your own replacements for what's left of this shift."

The three filed out, looking everywhere but at her, before the door slid shut behind them.

"Don't be too hard on them. They were just doing their job." Kai's scratchy voice shot down her spine on a shiver, and she turned to face him, grabbing onto the edge of the gurney before her jelly legs pitched her flat on the floor.

"Kai, I'm so sorry—"

He shook his head, and then pushed himself up on his elbows. "It's not their fault. Even I know the procedure when it comes to over-agitated patients."

She leaned over and hit the button to make the top half of the bed rise up.

"How can you be so understanding about this? They almost killed you. I mean, *Jesus, Mary and Joseph*, I had to restart your heart! If they'd read your chart thoroughly, they would have known—"

Kai reached out and snagged her hand. "I had another not-panic-attack and the nurses did what they were trained to do. The chart thing was an oversight, but people make mistakes."

She stared at him, taking in his pale complexion and the shadows in his eyes that might never go away, dark places in his soul she'd never be able to reach or comprehend. They were part of who he was now.

"I should go find Macaulay to come and check you over."

"Not yet." His grip tightened on her, his gaze dropping away. "I've been doing a lot of thinking. Hell, these days I don't have anything else to do."

She tugged against his hold, her skittering heart not able to take a deep-and-meaningful right in that moment. "Things are fine, Kai, you don't have to—"

He looked up sharply as he let her go, his gaze more resolute. "I'm not the same man I once was. I'm damaged goods. You could see that even when I couldn't admit to it."

"There might be parts of you that have changed, that won't ever be the same. But you're still my Kai; the guy I used to sit next to in history class back at pre-mil training, the one who used to pick the tomato out of his sandwiches at lunch time and give it to me because he knew I liked extra."

He dragged a hand across the lower half of his face. "No, that kid is gone. You deserve better than someone who is as messed up as I am."

The agitation tripped over into outright anger, and this time she was the one grabbing onto him. "Don't say that about yourself. You're still the most honorable man I've ever known, and no matter what the CSS did to you, that will never change."

He sliced her a glance heavy with regret and chagrin, his expression telling her he didn't believe a word she was saying.

"Part of my recovery is admitting that I'll never be the same, that I can't expect to live the life I once planned. I've decided to take that position they offered me, vice commodore, back on Earth."

Her heart took a plunging freefall, smashing into the bleak reality of his decision and what it would mean for them. Though she would know he was alive and well somewhere this time, she'd be lucky if she ever saw him again.

"Are you sure, that's a huge change in circumstance—"

Kai gave a single, resolute nod, his gaze unyielding and detached. "It's the best thing I can do for myself, and you helped me see that."

She looked away from him, swallowing over the tightness of her throat. It was almost funny that a week ago, this was what she'd demanded of him, yet now it was the last thing she wanted; it probably meant the end of their relationship in every sense of the word. Hard to maintain a close

Chapter Eighteen

Sacha leaned over the small sink in the medicos' communal room and splashed some cool water on her flushed face. *Jesus, Mary and Joseph.* She clenched her teeth and tightened her hands on the edge of the sink as another wave of nausea, backed up by dizziness, washed over her.

Whatever bug she'd caught, she was about ready to admit defeat, go home, and curl up on her uncomfortable couch in abject misery. But like the other couple of days she'd done that, she knew in another hour or so she'd be feeling fine again, like nothing had ever happened.

Just have to get through the next hour and I'll be okay…

"Sacha."

At the sound of someone calling her out in the corridor, she wiped a hand over her face and then groped for a towel. The door behind her slid open and she forced a deep breath on herself before she turned around.

Cass strode toward her, face tight with concern. "Damn, Sacha, you're sick again?"

Her best friend came over and set a hand against her cheek with no warning at all, her manner brisk and nurse-like as she checked her over. No wonder Kai had always complained about her acting like a doctor around him; it was damned annoying. She stepped back and shot Cass a glare as she patted the towel over the sweat dampening the back of her neck under her ponytail.

"I'm fine, Cass, it's just one of those bugs that sticks around longer than it has any right to. I'm sure I'll be better by tomorrow. In fact, I'm sure by this afternoon I won't even remember this happened."

Cass sent her an exasperated look, before taking a diag-pen from her pocket; a neat little device that could diagnose a range of ailments from a person's saliva. Her friend held it up, but she crossed her arms and sent Cass a stubborn look.

"I don't need you to check me—"

"You were sick this time yesterday."

She gave up on fending Cass off as wooziness assaulted her again. She pressed a hand to her forehead and winced. "So?"

"And you were sick about the same time the day before. In fact, just before lunch every day this week."

"I appreciate the sentiment, but I have patients to see."

She rolled her eyes and shoved the diag-pen toward her. "Did you sleep through half of medical training? If your sickness is due to what I think it is, you won't be any better tomorrow."

She gave up resisting and let Cass stick the absorbent tip

in her mouth like an old-fashioned thermometer. Her friend stepped back again and crossed her arms, staring at her in expectant silence while the seconds ticked by. At last the device let out a series of four staccato beeps and she pulled it from her mouth to read the inset screen.

PREGNANT. FOUR WEEKS AND THREE DAYS GESTATION. DUE DATE: 17 FEBRUARY 2437.

She fell heavily against the hard metal rim of the sink behind her, the impact jarring her lower back.

Pregnant?

"From the expression on your face, I'm guessing I was right."

She looked up at Cass, who was regarding her with understanding and concern. She couldn't reply though, because shock had numbed her to her very core, and apparently stolen all higher reasoning from her brain. *Pregnant.* How could she be pregnant—?

But of course. She'd had her mandatory military-issue birth control implant removed when she and Elliot had decided to start trying for a baby. *And never had it put back in.*

In fact, until today, with everything that had happened in the past year and a half, she hadn't even thought about the damn thing. That one night she and Kai had spent together had obviously been at the exact wrong time of the month… or the right time, depending on which way she decided to take this news.

A wave of delayed shock quaked through her. *A baby… Kai's baby.* Like a levy breaking its banks, a floodtide of feeling washed through her, emotions she'd forced down and disregarded for the past few weeks.

"Maybe you should sit down for a minute." Cass came forward and grabbed her elbow, then steered her over to the table. "Let me see if I can scrounge up some ginger-root tea. I've heard that helps with morning sickness."

Cass went over to the beverage dispenser, and Sacha rubbed both hands over her face as exhaustion slammed her. In the two weeks since she'd had to restart Kai's heart from the reaction to the sedative, things between them hadn't improved. They'd seen each other at meal times out of habit more than a desire to be in each other's company. At least, that's what it felt like. Truthfully, she didn't want to spend her free time with anyone else.

After Elliot had died, she'd walled herself up and forced herself to not rely on anyone but herself. It had taken Kai's announcement that he was leaving the *Knox* for good to make her realize she didn't want to live that lonely kind of existence any longer.

Only a handful of days remained until Kai left for his new posting on Earth. She'd tried to talk to him about his decision, but the conversations had been strained and stilted, his resolution absolute that taking the promotion was the best thing for him. That he needed a fresh start.

Except he wasn't happy. She could see it in the tense set of his mouth, in the grim shadows in his gaze, and the desolate way he looked at her when he thought she wasn't watching.

He was still taking steps to get back on solid ground. If the dark smudges under his eyes were any indication, he wasn't sleeping well. The most innocuous, day-to-day thing could set off a panic attack in him, though he strove so hard to hide them. Mentioning any type of medication shut him down faster than hyper-cruise engines going cold. His thrice-weekly appointments with the shrink continued, but he didn't talk about it, and she didn't ask. She honestly couldn't say if it helped him or not.

This baby changed everything.

She wasn't at all sure how he'd take the news, but she couldn't keep it from him, couldn't let him leave in a few days without him knowing he would soon be a father.

"Here. I found ginger-root and lemon tea." Cass returned and set a steaming mug down in front of her. "It doesn't taste great, but try to drink as much of it as you can. It should help with the nausea."

She murmured a short thanks as she wrapped a hand around the mug and lifted it to blow some of the steam off the top. Cass sat down across from her with that look on her face, the one that said they were going to talk about things whether she liked it or not.

If she weren't feeling so damn sick, she probably would have made a hasty escape. Unfortunately, her unsettled stomach made sitting there and sipping the ginger-root tea the safer option, no matter what Cass had to say to her.

"So, I didn't know you were seeing anyone." Though the words were casual, she could tell by the look on her friend's face that she was playing dumb, and at least suspected who the father was.

"Are we seriously going to talk about this right now when I'm about two seconds away from puking my breakfast?" Even just talking about it made her feel worse. She took a hasty sip of tea, scalding the tip of her tongue.

"When else am I going to be able to corner you?" Cass grinned.

She grimaced before taking another sip of tea. "What do you want me to say?"

Cass leaned forward across the table. "It's Commander Yang, isn't it?"

She pressed her lips together, not wanting to voice the truth, since she could find herself in serious trouble if the wrong people found out about her relationship with Kai while he'd technically still been her patient. But Cass was her best friend and would keep her confidence.

She pushed back a few strands of hair and sighed, the sound filled with the emotions weighing her down the past few weeks. "This is a mess. My whole life has become this huge mess. How can I possibly bring a baby into that?"

Cass covered her hand. "Maybe it just looks that way from where you're standing. Maybe cleaning it up will be simpler than you think."

Sacha gave a short, desolate laugh. "Believe me, this is going to require an industrial-sized vacuum cleaner."

"Don't you think the commander will be happy to hear about the baby? I heard he's leaving for Earth. Don't let that change your decision. You've got plenty of other people in your life who can help you—"

She shook her head. "I hope he'll be happy about it, because this isn't something I can keep from him. But things between us are so broken, a baby is the last thing we should be bringing into the equation."

Cass's expression became guarded. "Are you saying you might consider termination—?"

"No!" Sacha pressed a hand into the middle of her chest, just the word making her heart pound. "That's not an option. These might not be ideal circumstances, but I'm not going to take such drastic measures."

Cass blew out a relieved breath and sat back. "Good, that's good. I wasn't prepared to be having *that* conversation."

She dropped her gaze down into her half-drunk tea. "It's mind-blowing, really. All those months Elliot and I spent trying to get pregnant and I spend one night with Kai—"

"Only one night?" Cass screwed up her face. "Well, no wonder you're both walking around looking so cranky all the time. One night was obviously not enough."

"Apparently it was more than enough, if this baby is any indication." She laughed, everything seeming ridiculous all of a sudden. She'd spent so many months numb, not grieving Elliot and not moving on from the fact that both he and Kai were gone. And then Kai had returned and revived her emotions with all the subtlety of a tactical ballistic missile. In order to cope, she'd tried shutting herself down again, focused on being his doctor and nothing more, to the point she hadn't been able to see reason, which only hurt both of them. In hindsight, it all seemed so simple; she should have simply let the emotions wash over her. Yes, they would have burned, but she would have emerged on the other side the better for it.

Instead, she'd probably destroyed their half-a-life-long relationship through stubborn and resolute blindness.

"So what are you going to do?" Cass asked quietly.

"The only thing I can do." She rolled the cup slowly between her hands, nervous and excited about what this massive change in circumstance would bring. "I'll tell him about the baby, and tell him the only thing I should have told him since the day he came back."

"Which is what?"

"That I love him." She focused on her friend's face, ignoring the urge to cry welling up within her. There would be plenty of time for that later. "And that I'm sorry I hurt him, and I'll do anything to fix everything between us. I just hope it's enough."

Cass sent her a misty smile, her eyes suspiciously wet. "If he's half as smart as I think he is, then he'll take you in a heartbeat."

Her chest squeezed around her lungs, cutting off her breath at the notion of resolving things so easily. "God, I hope so."

Cass's moment of emotion seemed to have passed, and an excited gleam lit her gaze. "Call him now."

"Now?" Well, there was no reason not to…

Still, a wave of apprehension made her light-headed as she pulled her comm out of her pocket. Or maybe that was the pregnancy hormones. Thankfully, the sick feeling had started to pass, whether it was due to the ginger-root tea or just the daily illness running its course.

She sent Kai a message asking him to meet her for lunch, and then she and Cass sat silently while they waited to see if he would reply.

Her comm beeped. Disappointment poured through her as she read his reply.

"He says he's too busy for lunch today, and will see me tonight for dinner."

"*Pft*!" Cass crossed her arms. "There's no way he'll be too busy to hear this news. In fact, you should go up to the command center now. I only wish I could see his face when you tell him. Take pictures, all right?"

She laughed as Cass stood. "Sure, I can just imagine how

impressed he'll be about that. Just hold that expression of dumbfounded shock while I take a photo for Cass."

"You got it." Cass shifted over to give her a quick hug. "I'm so happy for you, Sacha. You're going to make an awesome mom. And I am going to be fun Aunty Cass, who always turns up with new toys and treats to spoil the heck out of this kid."

"I'll look forward to that," she grumbled, returning the hug. "But you're right. I'm going to head up and see if I can catch Kai in the command center."

"I better get back to rounds. Let me know how it goes, okay?"

Once her friend had left, Sacha took a deep breath, fortifying herself for the coming conversation with Kai. After a moment, she carefully stood, waiting to see if the recently cured nausea was going to make a comeback. When it didn't, she took another breath of relief and headed out of the communal room, managing to get off med-level without anyone asking her for anything, which in itself was a miracle.

She made her way up to the command center in the middle of the ship and asked the guards manning the doors if she could see Commander Yang.

As she went over to a nearby couch to wait, her med-comm vibrated and she snapped it off her belt. The code read *Charlie-One*, which meant there'd been a major incident at the main base of operations on the ground. She abandoned all ideas of waiting for Kai, instead turning to run for the transit-porter.

As she made the transit just before the doors closed, she got Macaulay on her comm. "What're the details?"

"There's been some sort of explosion down on Ilari at the

main base. They need all available medicos onworld ASAP."

"What's the verdict on the injured?"

"No clear, official report, but it looks bad. There's a transport being readied on port level bravo, bay echo-five. We have to go now."

"Grab me an emergency response pack, and I'll meet you up there." She disconnected the call and tabbed the transit screen to go into the upper levels of the ship, instead of down to med-level.

A few moments later, the transit doors opened to the chaos of soldiers and medicos boarding the shuttle headed for the ground. She scanned the crowd for Kai, though logically he couldn't have gotten down here before her. Besides, now was probably the worst possible time she could tell him. Drop a life-exploding bomb and then go down into live action on Ilari? He'd have a coronary over it.

She rushed with Macaulay and the other medico staff onto the transport, worrying about Kai with every step she took. What would he do when he heard about the explosion? Would he demand to go down to Ilari as well? How would it affect him to be on the planet again? God, she hoped he'd stay on the ship and not risk any further psychological damage. Who knew what facing the CSS so soon would do to his precarious recovery?

Once she'd found a seat, she let out a sigh of relief that Kai wasn't among the other people packed onto the shuttle, hopefully because he hadn't been cleared for active duty. What if something happened to him before she got to tell him about the baby? He could still leave her for the posting on Earth when he learned the truth if he wanted, but at least she would know he was alive and safe somewhere.

Chapter Nineteen

Kai snapped a surgical mask into place as he followed medicos from the second wave of transports into the most damaged part of the complex. He'd gone in for one hell of an argument with Commander Emmanuel about coming down here. Technically the man wasn't his CO, and he'd told Emmanuel in a few succinct words that they didn't have the power to stop him. The commander had finally relented, but damned if the bastard hadn't cleared him for weapon use. And Emmanuel had sunk the boot in by adding he was allowed to attend to any administrative or non-combative duties he saw fit, but was forbidden from actively engaging the enemy.

His heart pounded and a chilled sweat crept along his spine, but he forced himself to concentrate on his surroundings, not letting himself get sucked into the vortex of gut-clenching bad memories of last time he'd been on Ilari.

No one could tell him what had caused the explosion,

if it had been an accident or deliberate attack, how many personnel were unaccounted for, or who was even in charge down here.

So far he'd only come across cadets and lower-ranked soldiers. He'd started getting the feeling that maybe all of the senior officers and soldiers who might have taken control of the situation had been caught in the blast. Which, to his mind, spoke of a calculated assault. Was this the next move from the CSS they'd been waiting for, ever since the fire on the *Knox*? They hadn't found any trace of the CS Soldier who'd been posing as a UEF military guard, and a lack of any other leads had made the last few weeks frustrating to say the least.

The building looked barely recognizable anymore, the passage no more than a cave of twisted, blackened metal and debris. Able-bodied soldiers were scurrying back and forth, some putting out spot fires while others searched for victims. So far, only a handful of people had been pulled out alive. Most were coming out dead.

In the bowels of the building where the explosion had originated, the roof had been blown clear off, but at least that allowed bright sunlight to stream in, making the search easier. Up ahead, he saw Sacha and Macaulay organizing the sub-doctors and nurses into methodical teams, sectioning up the site so that no corner would be missed.

Since he'd made the decision to take the promotion on Earth, he'd been trying to keep himself detached from her, maintaining the most platonic relationship possible. It had put a definite strain on their already tenuous friendship, and if not for the fact he'd wanted to spend as much time with her as possible—awkward as it was—before he left for

Earth, he would have simply started avoiding her altogether. It definitely would have been the easier option. But no, apparently he was a twisted son of a bitch who enjoyed spending time with the woman he wouldn't allow himself to have.

With every little way Sacha looked after him, another part of his heart gave way to her. Yes, he had his issues to deal with, but Sacha had helped him see that the CSS hadn't managed to destroy as much of him as he'd first thought.

At some point in the past few days, the realization had struck him that he could not live without her. Not an hour went by when he didn't think about seeing her, or kissing her, or about taking her to bed like he had a month ago. But he refused to disregard the vow he'd made to himself about going to Earth and getting his crap sorted out so he could return to her a better man.

He watched while she directed one of the nurses to a corridor branching out toward the other end of the building, aiming a flashlight ahead of herself as she disappeared into the shadowed passageway. His heart clenched, but he turned from where she'd walked away and surveyed the scene in front of him. He couldn't worry about her. She was doing her job. Just like she'd been doing for the past few years when she'd been with Elliot. Just like she'd been doing the last year and a half when neither he nor Elliot had been around.

Although the soldiers were doing their best, the search for survivors and moving of debris had a definite sense of chaos to it. Kai grabbed the nearest cadet and started organizing the kids into a calmer and more efficient approach.

He'd been working with the younger soldiers for about half an hour, and they'd found another survivor. Yet when someone handed him a hastily accumulated list of the deceased, his fear about the senior officers and soldiers was realized. Colonel Cameron McAllister wasn't on the list... yet. But, he couldn't dwell on the fate of his friend too closely, not if he wanted to hold his shit together.

"Goddamn it." He shoved a hand through his hair and handed the datapad back to the cadet who'd given it to him. The CSS were behind this. Somehow they'd gotten into this supposedly secure, class-A facility and planted a bomb. Another mole? For a second everything started closing in on him, his chest getting tight, gut clenching as a cold spike railroaded right through his spine. *So not the time to lose it.* He clenched his fists and forced the rising panic down. He'd slowly gotten better at controlling the attacks in the past two weeks.

One of the cadets started to ask him something, but the words were drowned out by a deafening *boom*, eclipsed by a burst of super-heated air that knocked him from his feet.

Ears ringing and head splitting, Kai pushed himself up before he even registered he'd ended up flat on the floor. Around him, for a second, there was absolute silence and stillness in the wake of the explosion, but then chaos erupted like a second blast wave. Some people scrambled to their feet and rushed for any opening that could get them outside, some moved to help others, while a few remained ominously still where they'd fallen.

He wiped ash and dust from his watering eyes and squinted, looking for the source of the detonation. It hadn't been in this room, because otherwise they'd all be dead.

Across the open space, smoke billowed out of a hallway, backlit by the orange glow of another fire. *The corridor Sacha had gone down.*

Sheer panic drove him across the room, and he stumbled

blindly over twisted furniture and careened into someone else trying to get out. When he reached the opening of the corridor, he couldn't breathe. Heat from the fire stole the very air from the atmosphere. He shielded his face from the radiant heat, feeling the stinging prickle across his exposed skin.

"*Sacha!*" His yell came out hoarse, barely audible above the roar and crackle of flames. Someone grabbed his arm and he wrenched away, turning in a wild swing to see Sacha's friend, Cassidy, standing next to him.

"Commander, we have to get these people out of here."

Kai pointed a shaking hand toward the yawning mouth of flame and smoke. "Sacha went down there."

Cassidy's lips pressed into a grim line, but she didn't look toward the inferno.

"I know. We can't help her while the building is burning. We have to clear everyone we can from this room."

Howling despair wrenched through him, making him want to fall to his knees and scream in desolate fury. Instead, he clenched his fists and nodded awkwardly, tearing his gaze from the impenetrable hallway and surveying the new chaos in front of him.

Cassidy reached down and squeezed his hand, and then moved off to help a sub-doctor with an unconscious cadet. The one who'd compiled the list of deceased. Kai squeezed his eyes shut for a second as panic twisted insidiously through him, making his eyes smart. *Please let that cadet just be unconscious... Please let Sacha be okay.*

More numb than he'd ever been, even when he'd been at his lowest in that godforsaken hell of a CSS prison, he made himself move forward and randomly chose a fallen body to examine. Male. Nurse. *Alive.* Nasty gash on the head. It was a start. Kai picked the man up, swinging the weight over his shoulder into a fireman's hold, and focused on getting as many people out as he could.

• • •

Sacha gasped in a lungful of air and then curled in on herself as a fit of coughing seized her throat and lungs. She rolled over on the grass and looked up toward the rear of the building she'd just come out of. Smoke billowed upward into the blue sky, flames thrashing in the broken windows and licking up toward what was left of the second level.

Jesus, Mary and Joseph. If she hadn't come out here trying to get a clear comm signal—

Her heart froze, becoming a chunk of ice in her chest as she pushed up on her elbows and took a wild, searching glance for the nurse she'd teamed up with. There were chunks of debris scattered across the once-pristine lawn, but nothing even close to human-sized. She scrambled to her knees, but a sudden spasm of nausea made her double over again, bringing up everything she'd been fighting to keep down all morning. By the time the gagging subsided, her chest was aching and her heart hammering a strained rhythm in her chest.

With a groan for the fact she hurt everywhere, she swallowed over the bitter bile and shoved unsteadily to her feet. She had to get back to the main part of the complex, had to find Kai.

Another round of retching threatened as her breath hitched. *Kai.* God. What if he'd been somewhere near that explosion? She'd caught a glimpse of him as she'd left the main room, where most of the rescue effort was concentrated. But who knew what he'd done after that?

She picked her way carefully out of the debris field and paused at a garden tap to rinse her mouth out and drink some water. Okay, not a top priority right now, but it made her feel better. She straightened, trying to work out if there was a way to get back around to the parade ground where the transport had set down without cutting through the buttressed set of offices and amenities. Her heart skittered at the thought of going in somewhere, only to be caught in another explosion.

There seemed to be no direct route, apart from going all the way around the fence perimeter. The buzz of an engine overhead made her pause. She looked up, expecting to see another rescue transport, but instead she saw a battered, smaller ship, the CSS emblem blazoned in yellow and red across the vessel's underside.

CS Soldiers in the compound? Though her mind had already come to the conclusion that two explosions weren't likely to be an accident, the sight of an enemy ship touching down without the slightest hesitation sent a spurt of fear tripping through her limbs, setting off a definite *flight* response in her brain.

Sacha spun to make a run for the fence line, and came face to face with three ragtag-looking soldiers jogging toward her, all armed and wearing a patch over their hearts that proclaimed their allegiance. She backed up a couple of stumbling steps, gaze darting for an escape, but they'd already seen her. With the ship landing at her back and three armed soldiers coming toward her, she didn't have anywhere to go.

Chapter Twenty

Kai crouched down next to the sub-doctor he'd just helped evacuate from the twice-blown-to-hell building that had once served as Ilari's onworld command post. He took in a ragged breath and then coughed at the raw catch in his throat from inhaling so much smoke and dust. Someone handed him a near-empty canteen of water. He took a mouthful, and then gave it to Sub-Doctor Moore sitting next to him.

Cassidy came over to join them, holding a hand out for Ace to pass on the water.

"How are you holding up, Commander?"

Kai scowled at the nurse. Like he was some green soldier who was going to lose his Cheerios over a few war wounds? "Fine. I'm sure there's a dozen other people who need you asking them more than me."

Cassidy didn't seem fazed by his abruptness, instead glancing around at the makeshift triage. "Any sign of Sacha?"

Kai shook his head and swallowed over the instant lump

that blocked his throat at the mention of her name.

"She's probably busy helping people and doesn't even have a clue we're worried about her. I'm sure she and the baby are just fine."

Kai's hand shot out and grabbed the nurse's forearm in a bruising hold. "*The what?*"

Cassidy blanched. "The baby. Her pregnancy. She just found out this morning. Last time I saw her, she was on her way up to the command center so she could tell you."

Kai's grasp loosened of its own accord, his limbs going weak as he dropped to sit heavily on the hard ground. The land beneath him seemed to lurch and he sucked in a panicked breath. Sacha had disappeared and possibly gotten caught in the second explosion, her and the precious new life they'd unknowingly created. His eyes stung, making his lungs seize on a pained breath. *Dear god…Sacha.*

"Oh my god, she hadn't told you yet, had she?" Cassidy swore like a hardened soldier and then launched into a stuttered apology.

"It's not your fault. We need to find her. *Now.*" Kai wiped a rough hand over his face and then looked up at the nurse.

"I'll get right on it and see if I can't snag a few others to help me."

As Cassidy grabbed Ace and hurried off, Kai lurched unsteadily to his feet and studied the chaotic buzz of medicos around him, looking for the familiar gleam of bronze-spun hair.

A commotion a few meters over snagged his attention. A couple of young cadets had armed themselves and were arguing with soldiers not much older. Though his emotional weariness left him with exactly no patience to deal with some hot-headed toddlers, he hauled his sorry carcass over to the group.

"What's going on here?"

The soldiers snapped to attention, while the armed cadets made only the slightest half-hearted gesture at acknowledging him.

"Commander Yang, sir, these cadets have unconfirmed reports that the CSS have infiltrated the compound. They plan to go on a search and destroy within command perimeter, sir," one of the soldiers reported.

"Unconfirmed my ass," an armed cadet argued back. "I saw the ship with my own eyes. It was looking to touch down on the other side of the building."

Cold rage pounded through Kai like furious waves breaking down a seawall. He held a hand out toward the young cadet. "Give me that gun, cadet."

The young recruit sent the soldier a thwarted glare as he handed the weapon over, but Kai ignored him to turn to the other soldiers and cadets who'd gathered nearby. *To hell with Emmanuel's orders.* Would the commander really expect him to send a bunch of young, green recruits after CS Soldiers who'd managed to blow up supposedly the most secure complex on Ilari?

"I want every able-bodied person armed up and headed for the other side of this building like yesterday. Move out people!"

His yell was met by a chorus of, "Sir, yes sir!" and then the orderly movement of troops falling back on their training routines.

Kai motioned for the cadets and soldiers who were already armed to follow him and then set out at a jog toward the next building over, mostly untouched by the explosions apart from the busted out windows. He might be risking another explosion, but he wasn't about to waste the precious minutes it would take to go around by the perimeter fence if it meant catching the CSS a-holes responsible for this mess.

The pounding echo of boot steps accompanied them as they ran through the empty building. It must have taken less than a minute, but the run through the eerily deserted, jumbled offices seemed to take too long.

At last they emerged on the opposite end. Even as Kai shouldered through the doors with his purloined gun at the ready, his mind was taking in the scene and assessing every angle.

One small CSS ship on the ground, three CS Soldiers armed to the teeth, and Sacha caught in the middle. His insides iced as his mind kicked into combative action. The soldiers and cadets with him fanned out into formation, flanking him and making up a solid line of reinforcement. But even with over a dozen soldiers, albeit green recruits as backup, a cold sweat bloomed on his lower back. His arms trembled as he fought to keep the weapon steady and trained on the enemy.

"Stand down. Drop your weapons. Do not make a run at that ship or we will open fire!" His yell echoed a harsh warning across the tight open space where the ship perched, sounding every bit as convincing as he needed it to be. But inside, his guts were pinching like this was his first tour of duty. Neither he nor his men would open fire, *they couldn't*, not with Sacha standing in the direct line of site.

Sacha, pregnant with my baby.

The three CS Soldiers turned toward him, and another

wave of disbelief punched him as he recognized the soldier from the ship, still wearing a UEF uniform, but with a patch on his chest claiming his true allegiance. *Son of a bitch.*

"I said stand down!" For a long second, utter stillness descended over the scene. Behind the three men, Sacha dropped to the ground and started belly-crawling her way out of range.

One of the CS Soldiers said something, impossible to hear at the distance he stood from them. But the manner of the three men changed, and he knew what was coming, even as the CS Soldiers set their line and opened with guns blazing, sending everyone ducking for cover. Everyone except him. Kai froze. Utterly lost contact with his limbs. *Move… move you moron.* He was an easy target, especially since all the other soldiers and cadets had used their good-god-given sense and found shelter.

Even knowing he'd be dead any second, his legs stayed rooted to the ground, so he did the only thing he could do. He couldn't risk letting off a spray of ammo, which would have been the quickest and easiest way to take the three out—Sacha wasn't fully out of range yet. Instead, he lined up one of the CS Soldiers and squeezed off a single round. The guy dropped, but Kai had gone on to autopilot and had already moved on to the second soldier. And then the third. And then there was no one else standing on the grass except him.

Mind still in automatic combat mode, he turned and lined up the battered shuttle, popping a couple of rounds into the hull. This caliber weapon from this distance wouldn't do much except send a message that anyone who tried to step off the ship would be greeted by a round of weapon fire to the head.

The ship lifted off with a backlash of whirling air, gaining altitude and clearing the buildings in the blink of an eye.

In the aftermath of the ship leaving, silence fell. Some of the cadets and soldiers started coming up from behind their cover to stare at him with wide eyes, varying expressions of awe and amazement on their faces.

Kai let the gun fall from his numb hands. A cold shudder ripped through him and he couldn't take his eyes off the CS Soldiers he'd dropped with three single rounds. With his whole body shaking so bad, how had he even lined them up, let alone hit them with three pot-luck shots? *Pot-luck. Nothing but chance.*

A warm hand closed around his bicep and he dragged his gaze up to find Sacha staring at him, her eyes wary.

"Kai, are you with me?"

Her touch, her voice, the slight hint of acacia and summer he got over the acrid stench of smoke, snapped something inside him and sensation came back at him in a dizzying rush.

• • •

Kai grabbed Sacha's shoulders and hauled her closer, tipping her off balance.

"You're *pregnant*?" His hoarse demand, shouted near the top of his voice, made her wince. *Oh no.* She'd been prepared to deal with a lot of reactions from him, but outright fury hadn't been one of them.

Tears welled in her eyes as she braced her hands against his chest to get her balance. "I'm sorry. I was planning to tell you when I got the comm about the explosion. Please, don't be angry, I know it's a shock but we can—"

"You're pregnant and you came down here, putting yourself and *my baby* in danger? Frigging Jesus, Sacha! I thought you'd gotten blown up. And then Cassidy told me I'm going to be a father. Do you know what I felt in that moment?"

Relief drained her anxiety away. He wasn't angry about the baby. And he didn't need to tell her what he'd felt, because she could see the shadows of utter desolation in his eyes.

"I'm sorry, Kai. I didn't think. I'd only just found out the news myself and then I got the message about the explosion. I snapped into doctor mode." And she had, too. The thought of the little person inside her hadn't crossed her mind when she'd walked onto the shuttle to come down here. Sharp, de-layed shock sliced through her, bringing a fresh wave of nau-sea, this one laced with bitter anxiety. What if she'd gotten injured and lost the baby? "Oh god, you're right, I should have thought about the baby first. I'd never have forgiven myself if something happened. It's going to take a while to get used to the idea of being a mommy."

His shoulders dropped and he blew out a long breath as the tension within him seemed to wind down a few notches. He leaned down to gently set his forehead against hers.

"So, you want to be a mommy? I mean, I know you want to be, but with me?"

Her heart lurched right up into her throat, bringing on the urge to sob all over him. *Had to be the pregnancy hormones*.

"I know it was the last thing either of us were thinking

about or wanting. But yes, the idea of having this baby *with you*... Nothing could make me happier." Her voice wavered on the last word.

Kai caught her mouth in a deep kiss, fraught with emotion that made the tears welling in her eyes spill over and down her cheeks.

After a moment, he pulled back to look at her, using his thumbs to wipe away her tears.

"What about your new posting on Earth?" She couldn't get the words out at much more than a whisper, the lump in her throat making it hard to talk.

Kai shook his head. "They'll have to find someone else to fill it, because there's no way in hell I'm leaving the *Knox*. Wherever you and the baby are, that's where I belong. I know I still have problems to work through, but trust me, Sacha, I can conquer anything if I've got you. Tell me you believe that."

"I believe that." The heavy sensation that had been dragging down her soul these past weeks lifted, buoyed by swift relief, as he pressed another kiss to her mouth.

"Are you sure about this? Because you don't look so happy."

She sniffed and gave a watery laugh. "Yes, it's just been a long day."

"Tell me about it." He hugged her hard against him, kissing the top of her head. "Come on, they've already started transferring the injured back up to the *Knox*. Let's catch a ride."

He wrapped a firm arm around her waist and she smiled up at him. He frowned at her in return.

"FYI, I'm not letting go of you for at least a week. And

then I'm definitely not letting you out of my sight."

"That's going to make things in the bathroom a bit awkward." Though it was easy enough to make a joke, the weight of everything that had happened between them hung in the air. They still had more than a few issues to talk through, but the wall between them had collapsed, leaving her with the feeling that they could get through anything, as long as they did it together.

Before he could say anything in reply to her attempt at a jest, two of the cadets stepped into their path, followed by a couple of soldiers, until a large group of young people stood in front of them, all staring at Kai.

She looked up at him and caught the fleeting flash of panic in his gaze before he clamped his lips together and made his expression distant.

"What is it, soldier?" He directed the question at the nearest recruit.

The young man jerked a salute. "Commander, sir, it was an honor to witness you in live action and see that none of the stories we've heard of you were exaggerated, sir."

His entire body tensed against her, every muscle flexing until he became like a rock standing next to her. "I was just doing my duty, soldier, the same as any man. Now let's get back to the rescue efforts."

"No, it was more than that," one of the younger cadets piped up, earning a murmur of agreement from the others. "I've never seen anything like it in my life! When those CSS bastards started shooting, you just stood there as if you had ice water in your veins, calm as anything, and picked them off. You were invincible!"

A clamor of excited chatter broke out as each soldier

started relaying what they'd seen from their vantage point, but Sacha felt the slight tremble of Kai's taut body. The anxious gleam returned to his gaze. Whatever had or hadn't happened, he had reached the end of his endurance. He didn't seem to have a response for the crowd in front of him, just stood there staring at them all, his fists clenched so hard his knuckles were white.

Sacha let him go to step forward and then edged in front of him, planting her hands on her hips. "You heard Commander Yang. Are you going to make him repeat himself? There are injured men who still need rescuing and debris that needs clearing to help with the search effort. Why are you all standing around here yakking? Move it, recruits!"

The disorderly bunch of young soldiers and cadets hastily saluted and then started back toward the building they'd come through. Sacha rolled her eyes and then used her fingers to affect an ear-splitting whistle.

When the recruits paused and looked back, she pointed at the perimeter fence.

"Go around the buildings. And stay out of them until they've been cleared by the bomb team. I don't want to have to patch up any more of you because you were dumb enough to go inside and get caught in a third explosion."

A mumble of "Sorry, ma'am," rumbled from the crowd before the youngsters all jogged off toward the fence and then disappeared around the edge of the building.

She took a deep breath and then turned to look at Kai, but he had his gaze focused on the three dead CS Soldiers. His head moved slowly as he turned his attention to the gun he'd dropped on the grass.

"Kai, whatever's going on—"

All of a sudden he moved, stalking over to snatch up the gun from the ground. Her heart screamed to a stop and horror sliced through her chest.

What was he going to do?

She started forward, bitter cold dread propelling her to him. But before she could reach him, he disengaged the power clip from the weapon and put his whole body behind throwing it into the depths of the nearby garden. After that, he took the long nozzle of the gun and turned to smash it against a tree trunk over and over. A guttural, pained yell ripped from him, and then he hurled the damaged weapon the same way as the energy pack.

With a hand braced against the tree, his chin dropped to his chest and he slid down to his knees in a slow decent. His shoulders were heaving, but she didn't think he was crying. No, more like trying to get a hold of himself.

Sacha ran over and knelt down next to him, but didn't give in to the urge to touch him. He'd come to her when he was ready.

"I'm not a hero. I'm an idiot. A coward." The words came out choppy and broken over his uneven breath.

"I don't know what happened. I didn't see. I was too busy trying to get away. But whatever the recruits saw, it will be all over the *Knox* by shift's end today."

He covered his face with one hand as his head shook back and forth. "They think I bravely stood there and took down those CSS. But I *froze*."

His head jerked up and he looked at her. Tears wet his face, but he looked pissed, not upset. "Everyone else went for cover and *I froze*. Just stood there like a moron. The only reason I didn't get shot is because the CS Soldiers had lousy aim. I should be dead. I'm not fit for active duty. What if I'd died? What if *you'd* died? You and the baby?"

He started shuddering again, and she could see the panic digging deep claws into him. Sacha gave up on allowing him space and caught his face in her palms.

"It's all right, Kai. None of that happened. You might have had a second of hesitation, but then you acted and saved us all. It doesn't matter what everyone else thinks. All that matters is we survived and we're together."

He blew out a long tattered breath and wrapped both arms around her to drag her into his chest. He buried his wet face against her neck and she smoothed a comforting hand over his hair.

"If you're not fit for active duty today, it doesn't matter. Maybe you will be next week, or next month, or next year. Maybe you'll never go back into live action. It doesn't make a difference to me. We'll work things out one day at a time."

He laughed a sad, but relieved sound. "God, I love you."

She pulled back and urged his head up so she could look into his glistening, topaz gaze. "I love you too, Kai. I always have and I always will."

Epilogue

Sacha moved her fork half a millimeter to the left and then stepped back to admire her handiwork. She wasn't some domestic goddess, not by far. Heck, she could barely cook eggs. Tonight's dinner hadn't come from spending hours slaving in a kitchen. Actually, someone had slaved in a kitchen, but it hadn't been her. She'd simply commed one of the nicer takeaway restaurants and ordered up a meal for two.

But her table setting, well, that was damn fine.

The door to the apartment whooshed open and she skirted the table to walk into the sitting area. Kai had stopped by the hall table to shrug out of his uniform jacket. He ran a hand through his hair as he turned to her.

"How did it go?" She'd never been a hand-wringing type of person, but right then she was twisting the hem of her shirt into a mess.

Who could blame her, though? After the scene down on Ilari the day before, Kai had contacted the appropriate channels to tell them he'd changed his mind about the posting on Earth, leaving him in jobless limbo again. However, once the story of his actions on the ground had gotten back to Commander Emmanuel and Captain Phillip, they'd come to the conclusion that his fate needed to be decided right away. That, and he had to be court-martialed over disobeying orders.

A hastily convened court had been put together in less than twenty-four hours. He hadn't wanted her to go. And since she'd put in for leave from work, she'd been wandering around all day, stressing over what his fate would be. When she hadn't been throwing up, that was.

He undid the first three clasps on his shirt and pulled his tie free as he came toward her. "Well, I'm here, so obviously they didn't lock me up for arming myself and actively engaging the enemy when I'd been ordered not to."

She frowned and walked across the sitting area to meet him. She went into his arms and sighed in contentment. A small part of her had been worried he wouldn't come home tonight.

"So, stop dragging things out and tell me the verdict already. All this worrying can't be good for the baby."

He smiled down at her. "They've decided we need a more concentrated show of force on Ilari. In fact, they're sending in another battleship. *Farr Zero* is already en route. They want a permanent commander on the ground, instead of one whose responsibilities are divided."

Dismay and dread curled through her as she remembered him the day before. *I should be dead. I'm not fit for active duty...*

"They didn't give you the ground command, did they?"

He gave a short laugh and kissed her on the forehead

before stepping back and heading over to the table.

"Hell no! No way would I have taken that, even if they'd offered. Wow, this looks great." He dropped into his usual seat and flicked out a napkin before settling it on his lap.

Sacha sighed and went to start serving their dinner from the warming trays the restaurant had sent the food up in. No matter what she said, he'd tell her in his own sweet time.

Kai folded his arms on the edge of the table and watched her arrange food on their plates. "So there's actually going to be three commanders stationed at Ilari. One on the ground, one on the *Knox,* and of course Commander Buckley on the *Farr Zero.*"

She paused with the serving spoon hovering in midair, hope and happiness bursting through her.

"And...?" she prompted when he just sat there grinning at her.

"And...I get my old command back. Commander Yang will be taking charge of the *Valiant Knox* as of oh-nine-hundred tomorrow, while Emmanuel will be taking the ground command. But I'm on ship-bound tasks only. I won't be needed for active duty on the ground."

Sacha dropped the spoon into one of the bowls and threw her arms around his neck. Dizzying relief speared through her.

"And you'll be okay with that? The fearless Commander Yang not taking the CSS on in direct battle any longer?"

He shrugged and pulled her into his lap. "Let's face it, I'm getting on in years."

She laughed. "Yeah, you're doddering."

"And with a family to think of now," he continued, ignoring her teasing, "engaging in live action wouldn't be the smartest thing I've ever done. For the first time in my life, I'm going to put my heart before my career." He laid a large, warm hand over her still-flat belly. "And that means you and our baby are the most important things."

A lump of emotion made swallowing hard as she leaned down to kiss him.

"Anyway, being a hero isn't all it's cracked up to be." Though the statement might have been on the flippant side, Sacha saw the dark shadows pass through his golden gaze. Darkness that would remain there for the rest of his life.

"And while I might have broken orders, I did stop the CSS who'd planted the bombs from escaping. Emmanuel got told twenty different versions about how I didn't flinch when the enemy started shooting and stayed cool and calm in taking them out. We both know it's a load of rubbish, but Commander Emmanuel wants to give me some award for bravery in the line of fire, or some crap." He made a face. "I don't want an award, another ribbon to pin on my chest. I just want to forget the whole damned day happened."

Sacha hugged him against her chest as he sighed. Her gaze strayed up to the display cabinet where the bronze medal set with a yellow ribbon glinted softly under the lights. Kai needed to know about that little talisman, but not tonight. One day in the future, when time and distance put him in a better frame of mind about things.

And then something occurred to her. "Hang on, we can't forget the *whole* day."

He glanced up at her and smoothed a hand over her hair. "Why the hell not?"

"Because yesterday we also found out we were going to be parents."

"Oh yeah. *God.* As if that just doesn't make every damned single thing a whole lot better." He looked down at her stomach and a loving smile lit his features.

The tender expression knocked the breath right out of her, and for about the millionth time, she thanked the Lord that miraculously, Kai had come back from the dead.

"I'm glad you came home, Kai."

His gaze came up to meet hers and then he kissed her gently. "I might have gotten out of that prison on my own, but you've saved me every day since. I didn't just come home, I came home to you."

THE END

Acknowledgments

As always, thanks to my critique partner and mentor, Erin Grace, even though we're both so busy these days, we don't get as many chances to talk like we used to. You still always tell me like it is, and I know you're there if I ever need anything, especially a synopsis!

Lisa, thank you for seeing what I couldn't and helping me bring out the final shine in this book.

Thank you so much to Robin—the most wonderful editor in the world—we've worked together so well, and ever since the first day you emailed me, you've been so positive, enthusiastic, and encouraging about my work. The editing process can be stressful, but you made it seem like a breeze. And to Stacy, thank you for reinforcing Robin's confidence in my work, and for the suggestions you made that turned this book into what it is now. This has definitely been a team effort, one that I have immensely enjoyed being a part of.

Also, a big thanks to the rest of the Entangled team that

helped get this book out into the world.

As always, thanks to my agent, Paula, for all the time and work she's put into me, both with Entangled and my other books, even the ones we've had to put aside. It's all been valuable experience, and I hope we continue building a solid foundation together for many years to come.

Lastly, Mario, thank you isn't enough. We make a great team, and we've created a beautiful family. I might not always say so, but everything you do—from taking the kids and not complaining when I disappear behind my computer, to cleaning the bathrooms because you know how much I hate doing that—I notice every detail and wonder how I got so lucky to share my life with you.

About the Author

Jess has been making up stories ever since she can remember. Though her messy handwriting made it hard for anyone else to read them, she wasn't deterred and now she gets to make up stories for a living. She loves loud music, a good book on a rainy day, and probably spends too much time watching too many TV shows. Jess lives in regional Victoria, Australia, with her very supportive husband, three daughters, one ball-obsessed border collie, and one cat who thinks he's one of the kids. Learn more about Jess at www.jessanastasi.com

3104

Made in the USA .
Columbia, SC
04 April 2018